ANKLE BREAKER

ANKLE BREAKER

A NOVEL BASED ON A TRUE STORY

MARGARET JANE BROWN

©2022 by Margaret Jane Brown. All rights reserved.
Published by Redemption Press, PO Box 427, Enumclaw, WA 98022.
Toll-Free (844) 2REDEEM (273-3336)

Redemption Press is honored to present this title in partnership with the author. The views expressed or implied in this work are those of the author. Redemption Press provides our imprint seal representing design excellence, creative content, and high quality production.

No part of this publication may be reproduced, stored in a retrieval system, or transmitted in any way by any means—electronic, mechanical, photocopy, recording, or otherwise—without the prior permission of the copyright holder, except as provided by USA copyright law.

Many of the names and places used are real, while some are made up. The author has received permission from those living to include them in this novel.

ISBN 13: 978-1-64645-778-6 (Paperback)
　　　　 978-1-64645-780-9 (ePub)
　　　　 978-1-64645-779-3 (Mobi)

LCCN: 2022916225

For Marty, whose story leads me and so many others.

Two things make a story.
The net and the air that falls though the net.

—Pablo Neruda

Contents

Cheers ix
Prologue New Hampshire, Christmas 2009 xi
Chapter 1 Crossover Sacramento, 1974 13
Chapter 2 Arkansas, October 2002 Twenty-Six Years after the Murder 19
Chapter 3 Blindsided Sacramento, August 1974 21
Chapter 4 Arkansas, August 2002 Twenty-Five Years after the Murder 35
Chapter 5 Fifty-Six to Six Sacramento, December 1974 39
Chapter 6 Sacramento, 2002 Twenty-Five Years after the Murder 51
Chapter 7 Anger Management 55
Chapter 8 Sacramento, 2000 Twenty-Three Years after the Murder 63
Chapter 9 Fearless 65
Chapter 10 Sacramento, 1999 Twenty-Two Years after the Murder . 77
Chapter 11 Shuttle Play 79
Chapter 12 Who's Next? 95
Chapter 13 Sacramento, 1998 Twenty-One Years after the Murder 103
Chapter 14 Bust off the Bench 105
Chapter 15 Chasing the Hot Dog 117
Chapter 16 Arkansas, 1994 Seventeen Years after the Murder 123
Chapter 17 David and Goliath 125

Chapter 18 Sacramento, 1978 Six Months after the Murder 139
Chapter 19 Hustle Points 141
Chapter 20 Sacramento, 1977 Two Months after the Murder.....149
Chapter 21 Foul Trouble 153
Chapter 22 Sacramento, May 11, 1977 Four Days after the
    Murder 161
Chapter 23 Inconceivable..165
Chapter 24 May 9, 1977 Three Days after the Murder 179
Chapter 25 Ankle Breaker 181
Chapter 26 Heart Breaker Sacramento, May 1977 187
Chapter 27 Overtime Sacramento, 1980 193
Author's Note 197

Cheers

My gratitude starts, as usual, with Marty. "I saw the crescent; you saw the whole of the moon."

To Megan, Kat, and Micah—you are at the core of my heart. Thank you for being the jewels in my crown—if I had a crown.

Thank you to my sister, Cindy, who always, and I mean always, has my back. Thank you for the painstaking work of research. I appreciate so much those trips to downtown Sacramento, rummaging around in newspaper archives.

Thank you to Pete Willover for sharing this story with a complete stranger. I think your career would be a true-crime best seller.

To Gerry Willmett—eternal thanks to a true lifelong friend and stalwart man of God.

Thank you, Bill Colton, my expert kids' basketball coach and endearing friend.

Thank you to Kate Schafroth for reading, editing, and all those salmon-hash breakfasts.

Thank you to the Inklings. I heard Winnie the Pooh say, "It is more fun to talk with someone who doesn't use long, difficult words but rather short, easy words like, 'What about lunch?'"

To my Boise fan club, Tim and Renee Rule and Bill and Laurie Pubols—thank you for reading the book and encouraging me to keep at it. Please read the finished product—it is much better.

Thank you to Lesley McDaniel, my editor, teacher, and new best friend.

To fall in love with God is the greatest romance; to seek Him the greatest adventure; finding Him the greatest human achievement.

—Augustine

Prologue

New Hampshire, Christmas 2009

Marty stared out the window as the snowplow shoveled up snow and piled it on mounting drifts for the second time that day. The winter storm had been relentless. Snow had fallen for days, and it wasn't letting up.

"Christmas in New Hampshire sounded like a good idea when I got the tickets a few months ago." Marty spoke out loud as he looked down at his phone for word of the arrival of his adult children.

He and his wife, Margaret, had just moved to the cozy "empty nest" condo in New Hampshire to begin working with a ministry in Boston. They waited restlessly while their kids battled their way through airports, to rental car agencies, and along icy roads. Christmas travel across country—never a good idea.

Twenty-year-old Micah arrived first from Portland, Oregon, where he attended college. Middle daughter, Kat, reached New Hampshire from Phoenix in flip-flops. Megan and her new husband, Jesse, flew in from Spokane, Washington, where the weather wasn't much better.

The tree was up; a fire blazed in the fireplace; popcorn and eggnog were laid out on the counter. Micah and Jesse set up Red Alert to play on their laptops, and the girls switched on the TV and hit pay dirt with a *Cold Case Files* marathon.

Everyone's attention was drawn to the TV when, after a few episodes, they realized they had lived in all the places where the grisly murders took place.

There was the bludgeoned body found in the wilds of Montana, where all three kids were born. Another episode depicted the horrific murder that took place close by in a remote town in Maine. And the story about the beaten body of a homeless man murdered in Phoenix, where Kat went to college.

As the next episode in their marathon began, they couldn't help but laugh. "Up next on *Cold Case:* teen murder in Sacramento." The town where Marty grew up.

Marty shot up off the couch. "No way!"

Startled, Margaret asked, "What?"

Riveted by a picture on the screen, he said, "I coached that kid! Really, you guys."

"Really?" Megan's face was a mix of curiosity and skepticism.

Marty gulped and continued to stare at the screen. "I've told you about the Johnson basketball team that I coached back in the seventies. I can't believe it!"

Marty sat back down on the couch, and they all turned their attention to the screen, a blast from the past that was blowing their minds.

"I was on this case from the day it happened." The caption on the screen identified the man speaking as Detective Pete Willover. "We had a good idea who did it, but we couldn't prove it. We wouldn't be able to prove it . . . not for twenty-six years."

When the segment ended, Margaret turned to Marty. "Okay, you've got to tell us the whole story." She reached for the remote and hit the pause button, then stood. "But we are definitely going to need more popcorn."

Chapter 1

Crossover
Sacramento, 1974

Coach Marty watched with admiration as point guard Duane Davis moved down the court, determined and composed. He stopped just past the half-court and continued to dribble the ball. Finally, he lifted it high with two hands and faked a pass over the head of his helpless opponent in the white jersey, who then turned to follow where he assumed the ball was headed. Duane then sent the ball directly to his teammate Demetrius who waited outside the key.

Confused, the white team dropped their guard and let Duane get positioned a few steps off the key in time for Demetrius to pass the ball back to him.

One lone white jersey remained in the key and rushed to guard Duane before he scored. Dribbling the ball with his right hand, he was able to draw the white jersey to Duane's right. He faked with a wide step to his right, then with lightning speed, he bounce-passed the ball to the other hand, stepped to the left, and shot the ball, sending the off-balance white jersey to the floor.

What only took a few seconds resulted in two points and the kid on the floor clutching his rolled ankle in agony. Unfortunately for Duane, the ref only saw the kid on the floor, blew his whistle, and stopped the game to call a foul on Duane.

The coach of the green team, Marty Brown, threw his hands in the air in protest. "Are you blind!" he yelled. "There was no foul! Come on!"

His team, the Hagginwood Hawks, were up against the St. Mary's Falcons. The Hawks had traveled across town to the burbs to play in the tournament.

Playing in green T-shirts dyed at home, the Hawks were a stark contrast to the St. Mary's team, who were decked out in new white jerseys with "St. Mary's" emblazed in red across their chests.

The Falcons' team parents ruled the bleachers, filling the gym to standing room only. The roar was deafening as the score remained close through the entire first half.

Marty was proud of his team. They worked hard and made improvements all season. They had won their league and dominated all their games in this NorCal twelve-and-under tournament, which had led to this final game.

Duane was the first to get in foul trouble. He was the best player, top scorer, and heart of the team. He could be a handful but was a remarkable athlete for a twelve-year-old.

Marty's six-foot, four-inch frame paced back and forth along the sideline. His full dark beard and thick dark brown hair reached past the collar of his T-shirt. He wasn't trying to look intimidating, but clenching a wadded-up roster in his hand helped control his frustration, which was mounting minute by minute.

The halftime buzzer sounded in the nick of time. Marty, saved from the inevitable confrontation with refs, drew a breath of relief.

The team sat down on the bench, exhausted.

"Listen," he said, kneeling in front of them. "You guys are killing it out there. You are doing all the things we learned this season—rebounds, speed, accuracy, heads-up ball. Everything I would hope for."

Looking at Duane, he said, "That ankle-breaker move was a thing of beauty. I don't think I've ever seen a sixth grader pull that off. I'm sorry the ref didn't see it that way, but it was classic. There was no foul but when that kid hit the floor, you were doomed."

Marty did his best to keep perspective and help the guys get calmed and focused. How he would calm himself, he wasn't sure. The crowd was biased; the score, unjust; the refs, blind. It felt impossible.

The second half only got worse. Marty took Duane out after three fouls to protect him from fouling out. But his next best players all had fouls of their own piling up. By the third quarter he had no choice. He put Duane back in, sat down Demetrius, and put in his sixth player.

In their desperate attempt to score, the Falcons were making hay on their free throws and Marty was left without options. First Duane fouled out, then Demetrius, then Manuel, then Damien. It was demoralizing.

By the start of the fourth quarter, there was one eligible sub on the bench, and Marty flew into a rage. "Come on, Ref!" he yelled. "Let's see some calls on both sides!"

The ref shot back, "Why don't you stick to coaching and we will do the refereeing!"

"Deal! How about if you do some refereeing!" he yelled as he ran down the sideline to keep up with the action.

Finally, another Hawks player, crippled with four fouls, was the victim of the ref's whistle. Marty stared at the man in total disbelief, then heard him call, "Green-12." The player walked off the court dejected, plopped down on the bench, and dropped his head in his hands.

The ref tossed the ball to a Falcons player, then blew the whistle again. "Hey, Coach. You only have four players on the court."

Unable to control himself, Marty rushed onto the court and headed straight for the ref. Every one of the Hawks stared in horror as they watched their coach totally lose it.

He towered over the man in the black-and-white striped shirt, and with every ounce of intimidation he could muster, he hollered, "You fouled out all my players! Your reffing sucks!"

Before he could spew out every demeaning insult he knew, he felt a pair of arms encircling him from behind.

"Coach!" a voice cried out. "Coach, remember what you taught us, man."

Marty looked back at the pleading eyes of Duane. "Come on, Coach, back to the bench. You would flatten that guy and then where would we be."

Duane's actions melted Marty's anger and he headed back to the sideline. Duane, easily the rowdiest player on the team, seemed much older than his twelve years would imply. This was the kid he had to sit on all the time—the kid whose foul language and antics on and off the court rivaled most high schoolers.

Walking back to the bench, Marty locked eyes with Duane's mother, who had stood up amid the hostile crowd. Her face said *thank you*, and in that moment Marty knew this was the genuine victory for the season.

He sat down on the bench and watched in vain as his four subs finished out the game. It would have been justified if they got up and walked out of the gym and had not looked back, maybe slashing a few tires in the parking lot. But they didn't; they finished the game. The starters, now on the bench, kept their heads up and encouraged their teammates until the end.

Marty lay in bed that night, well past midnight, brooding over the game. He relived every play, every basket, every unjust call from the refs. He knew he would remember it, play-by-play, for the rest of his life.

He had tried to keep things simple, prioritizing the basics.

These kids were athletic, but it was hard work to help them hone skills, focus, and learn plays.

The other priority was sportsmanship. Twelve-year-olds—notorious for complaining and blaming—often gave up when things didn't go their way. He hammered away at the importance of a positive attitude, respect for others, and playing as a team, not to mention having fun.

The pressure is on for these kids, he thought. Identities were being shaped. As a coach, good or bad, he understood the impact sports had on how kids viewed themselves and everyone else. Marty never took that influence for granted.

His own years of sports proved the point. He thought about his high school football coach that cracked a clipboard over his head. Or the basketball coach that falsely accused him of cheating on a math test and cut him from every basketball team for the rest of high school. That deep dread of failure and constant pressure to be someone permeated every game. *Sports should help not hurt!*

He rolled over and stared into the darkness, wrestling with the growing uncertainty over whether he should keep coaching. *I was losing it out there today, and it took a twelve-year-old delinquent to keep me from punching that ref.*

Finally, he decided it would be good to take the next year off from coaching and focus on school. *That ought to be enough stress to manage,* he decided as he drifted off.

Chapter 2

Arkansas, October 2002
Twenty-Six Years after the Murder

He relished the stillness of his dilapidated home, even though it was a broken-down cabin in the woods. Everyone was gone: ugly wife, snot-nosed brats, hounding cops. All quiet for the moment. He wheeled himself over to the closet, now void of ugly wife's crap, reached in, and grabbed the fully loaded T/C .22 automatic that stood against the closet wall. He always kept it loaded because if he needed it, he didn't want to waste time scrambling around for bullets.

He laid it across his lap, rolled back to the living room window, and opened the curtains for a look. After using the rifle to break through a pane, he rested the rifle on the jagged windowsill, pointing at the gravel drive in front of his cabin. He listened for a moment, heard nothing, then decided he needed a beer.

He put the rifle back on his lap, turned the wheelchair around, and headed for the fridge. His frustration mounted as he found it empty of anything but moldy hot dogs. He swore out loud and punished the appliance with a slam that rocked it off its feet.

He backed up again and turned, looking around the room for a cigarette. Spotting an empty tuna can filled with butts, he wheeled over to it and picked out the longest one. Maybe a drag or two would calm his nerves. He put it in his mouth, searched the room for a match, and spotted a small wooden matchbox on the mantel over the cold stone fireplace. He wheeled over, grabbed a poker, and knocked the box into his lap, only to find it empty. He threw the box with force into the fireplace along with the cigarette stub.

A search through the cupboards, drawers, and shelves produced no liquor, no joints, no cigarettes, not even a match to burn the place down—nothing to soothe his mounting desperation. He had always been able to calm himself, always been able to get himself out of situations like this, but not today. He headed for the window with the rifle in his lap, then stopped short when he heard the familiar whining of police sirens.

They were getting close. There was more than one. It sounded like every cop in the county was on the way. They were coming for him. He loved his .22, a reliable friend, but not today. No way would a gun in the window get him out of this mess. So many messes, so many close calls and escapes and lies. But not today.

He backed up the wheelchair to the middle of the room and positioned the rifle between his legs with the butt on the floor, the barrel pointed at his chin. He waited until they were at the door, pounding, calling his name.

The crack of the rifle echoed from the cabin, through the woods, ending the twenty-six-year search for Dean Jennings.

Chapter 3

Blindsided
Sacramento, August 1974

Marty shifted the pickup into third gear and made his way up the deserted avenue. It was not yet dawn, and the temperature had cooled to a barely livable one hundred degrees. With the windows rolled down, he felt sweat already trickling down his neck. His beater truck struggled to move fast enough to create a breeze through the windows.

Finals week had ended and, mercifully, his first year of college was over. It had been brutal. The disappointment of not getting into his first choice of colleges, compounded by the injury that ended his walk-on career on the Sac State basketball team, made the year a hard one. Losing that game in the NorCal Tournament probably was the biggest hit to his confidence. So here he was, delivering papers to paperboys in the middle of the night.

Volunteer work as a coach was fun most of the time, but the emotional toll was rough. Refs drove him crazy. He liked the solitude of the night shift, that was for sure.

His dream of becoming a park ranger in the wilds of the California Sierra Mountains was now dashed because of his failure to get into a forestry program, ending his notion of the idyllic life of solitude in a fire tower high above the pines.

He shifted into fourth gear and picked up speed on the deserted street. His mind pondered the decision to take the night shift job that paid the bills and allowed daytime hours for class. Solitude minus the view.

Out of the silence of the half-light, he heard a whining motor to his right. A motorcycle at top speed came down a hill straight for the intersection he had just entered. With no time to stop, Marty braced for the collision. Then, after what felt like a scene from a slow-motion action film, the motorcycle slammed into the pickup, projecting its rider over the hood of the truck and onto the pavement. Marty watched in horror as the rider skidded across the pavement, landing on the other side of the road.

Heart pounding, Marty stopped the truck and jumped out. He ran to the rider and found him face down, dressed in black with his head covered by a ski mask.

Moving with caution toward the man, he asked, "Hey, are you okay? Man, you came out of nowhere. You must've been going ninety!"

With no response, he took a few tentative steps closer and noticed, out of the corner of his eye, a pistol lying on the ground. Instinctively, he kicked the pistol as far away as he could.

Before he could discern what to do next, he heard sirens. Faint at first, then louder and coming from the same direction as the masked motorcycle rider. Looking up, he saw the police cars careening down the hill, headed straight for him.

The first police car flew into the intersection and came to a stop next to Marty's pickup. Two more followed, filling the intersection with lights and deafening sirens.

The police rushed from their cars and ran to Marty, who was standing in the street.

"He had a gun!" Marty pointed to the weapon he had kicked away. "He came screaming down that hill out of nowhere."

Trying to explain what happened, his heart thundered. "Is he dead? That guy came out of nowhere. He hit the side of my truck, landed over there, and hasn't moved. He must have been doing ninety! Is he dead?"

The officer knelt beside the body and felt for a pulse. "No, he isn't dead. He's screwed, though."

A second officer finished calling for an ambulance and walked to Marty, who stood frozen in the street. "You okay, man?" he asked. "That guy robbed a 7-Eleven." He put a hand on Marty's shoulder. "Thanks for your help," he said with a grin.

Marty looked at him with disbelief. "I could have killed him! He ran right into my truck and flew over the hood. I've never seen anything like it!"

As the two men stared down at the unconscious robber, the officer said with some reassurance, "You probably saved his life. Hitting your truck like that stopped a big chase that wouldn't have ended well."

Marty couldn't take his eyes off the frail, black-clothed figure. The officer had removed the ski mask, and the unconscious criminal lay exposed on the street. He was young and innocent looking in that moment.

The stress of the last few minutes lessened as Marty stood alone in the middle of the road. He watched as the paramedics put the kid who hit his truck on a stretcher and wheeled him to the safety of the ambulance.

"Do you need the docs to look at you?" A voice broke the silence of the surreal moment.

"Uh, I think I'm okay. Shook up a little, but I'm okay," he said as he watched the ambulance drive away, sirens and lights fading down the street.

By now, the neighbors were out on their lawns, donned in robes and slippers. Enjoying the early morning drama, they stood around chatting as the police dealt with the crime scene.

Feeling light-headed, Marty leaned his back against the vehicle and slid to the ground and closed his eyes. A voice startled him back to reality.

"Geez, man, are you okay? What the heck happened? The police called rambling on about late newspapers. Are you okay?"

Marty looked up to the face of his boss, Jim, leaning down over him. "Some guy robbed a 7-Eleven and was trying to get away on a motorcycle. He collided with my truck."

"Are you kidding! Unbelievable." Looking at the scene, he shook his head. "You're lucky he didn't kill you, kid."

Lucky hadn't been in his thinking. He felt like a truck had hit him instead of that kid on the motorcycle.

Jim told him to go home and take the week off. "I'll take care of the papers for the week. I don't want you to worry about it."

Marty watched as his boss loaded up the papers into his own truck and drove off to make the deliveries to paperboys around the city who were probably already sitting on their doorsteps in the dark, waiting for Marty and their papers.

Left alone, with all the excitement dissipated, he started the engine of the banged-up, already crappy truck, and headed for home. The first thing to do: call Gerry and head to the mountains.

Try as he might, he couldn't stop the sound of the screaming motorcycle and the crunch of metal from repeating in his mind like a stuck record. He couldn't stop hearing the sirens or forget the recurring vision of the black-clad body flying over the hood of his car.

So many questions swirled around in Marty's head as he and Gerry set up camp.

What if he had not been unconscious? What if he had used the gun to get away when I went over to see if he was all right? What if he gets off and then comes looking for me?

The questions rang in his ears like the sirens of the police cars.

It would take days to calm down and try to forget about it. Would a few days in the mountains get the entire thing out of his head?

As his freshman year ended, he had already been asking a lot of unanswerable questions. *What am I doing? Why put so much work into school when I can't go where I want or study what I want? What if I'm only good for dead-end jobs? What if I died suddenly? Would anyone care?*

The questions—rational and irrational—spun around in his head. He watched Gerry, his best friend through high school, move around the camp without a care in the world. He was a fun-loving guy, albeit kind of dorky. His jet-black hair and short, muscular frame made the two look like Mutt and Jeff, a reference only their parents could appreciate.

"What is this?" Marty asked as he pulled out a cedar chest full of food for their week in the Sierras.

"My sister's hope chest," Gerry answered absently.

Marty looked at him in disbelief. "You emptied Sue's hope chest and filled it with food? Are you crazy? She'll kill you!"

Gerry shrugged and pulled out a tent from the back of the car and proceeded to get the camp set up.

Later that night, when the two were in their sleeping bags, Marty could finally relax a little. He had been functioning on a lot of adrenaline since the accident that morning. He took a deep breath and secretly hoped Gerry didn't want to chat. Gerry always wanted to chat. Marty wanted to sleep, just sleep, and forget the day had ever happened.

He waited for the soothing sounds of the woods to lull him to sleep. Instead, he heard a low growl from across the campsite, then a banging noise that sounded like large objects landing in the dirt. They both popped up and tried to figure out what they were hearing.

"Is that a bear?" Gerry asked.

"Shut up! He probably just wants our food."

After hearing the distinct pop of the ice chest lid busting open, they swallowed hard at the eerie screech of claws across the smooth shellacked surface of the cedar hope chest.

Gerry chose that moment to confess. "Oh no, all my sweets and snacks are in here!"

An uncharacteristic expletive shot from Marty's mouth like a bullet. His body tensed as he willed himself not to reach over and punch the guy for his stupidity.

Gerry looked at his friend with severity. "Marty, you know you shouldn't take the Lord's name in vain like that."

"Are you kidding me?" He shook his head in disbelief. "There is a bear out there, and you are worried about swearing?"

The adrenaline spike, for a second time that day, caused his heart to pound wildly, and fear gripped him like a vice. There was nothing but the cheap canvas tent separating them from what could be a very gruesome end.

He froze, listening to the unnerving sound of the huge animal's heavy breathing on the outside of the tent and considering the possibility of human sacrifice for a half-eaten bag of Fig Newtons.

After what seemed like an eternity, they heard the bear move away from the tent, and finally, their campsite. With flashlights in hand, they inched silently through the camp, picked up what remained of their supplies, and loaded them in the car.

"Do you think we can get any sleep in here?" Gerry asked as he tried to get comfortable in the back seat.

It was only seconds before Marty heard his friend's soft snore.

For Marty, sitting up in the front seat, sleep didn't come. The accident that day and the rummaging bear left him with an overwhelming sense of doom.

How could Gerry sleep? Every muscle and fiber of Marty's being was on edge, made worse by an anxious dread that his life didn't matter.

Early the next morning, the two crept out of the car to survey the damage. Revived by the deep scent of pine and the stillness of the woods, Marty felt a little better. The ice chest that had held their food lay dented and empty. The hope chest had survived the attack but would forever display the evidence of the bear's impressive claws.

The park ranger made an appearance and confirmed that a black bear had wandered through the campground. "You boys had to learn the hard way why we always say to leave your food in your vehicle," he said grimly.

He left them to ponder what they would eat for the next few days. Oddly enough, they didn't consider going home. It was all kinds of depressing.

"Gerry let's go for a hike," Marty said, trying to take his mind off the meager breakfast of hot dog buns and chips.

"Maybe later," Gerry said as he reached for a book in his pack.

"A swim? How about a swim?" Marty suggested.

Gerry looked at his friend and said, "I'd be up for that in a little while."

Marty looked at him with frustration, "Well, let's do something! I didn't come out here to sit around."

He realized immediately that he was overreacting. The night in the front seat of the station wagon left him tired, hungry, and massaging an irritating kink in his neck.

Gerry opened the thick paperback that he had retrieved from his pack. "I like to start my day by reading a few chapters out of the Bible," he said without looking up.

The Bible? Marty discreetly rolled his eyes. *Since when did his crazy, prankster, goof-off friend read the Bible?*

Marty succumbed. "Okay, sorry. Let's do that then." He plopped down on the bench of the picnic table next to Gerry and waited to see where this dumb idea would lead.

Gerry flipped through and chose a poem. Marty hated poetry.

Poetry in the Bible sounded like the worst kind of poetry. At first, he read about protection from harm in what sounded like war. "A thousand may fall at your side, ten thousand at your right hand, but it will not come near you. You will only observe with your eyes and see the punishment of the wicked."

"Hmm," Marty said out loud as he pictured the black-suited rider flying across the hood of his car.

Gerry continued. "If you say, 'The Lord is my refuge,' and you make the Most High your dwelling, no harm will overtake you, no disaster will come near your tent."

"Whoa!" Marty exclaimed as he looked at his friend. "Did you make that up?"

"No," Gerry said with a little laugh. "I swear it's right here. This is the Psalm for the day."

"That's weird," Marty said, staring at the page. It did not go unnoticed that it was the first time he had ever seen the actual inside of a Bible. Someone gave him one a few months before, and he had laughed at the notion of ever reading it.

Gerry flipped back a few pages. "I read Psalm 90 yesterday, and today was 91! That is why I like to read every morning before I start my day. It is usually relevant, but that is right on!"

"Is that it?" Marty asked.

"Well, no," Gerry said. "I like to read a Proverb too. Let's see, today is the third, so let's look at Proverbs 3."

He read with Marty's rapt attention. "Trust in the Lord with all your heart and lean not on your own understanding, in all your ways submit to him, and he will make your paths straight."

"Cool" was all he could think to say.

The rest of the day brought blue skies and warm sun. The lake was cold and invigorating. A family from Reno invited the guys to share their dinner. They sat around a lively fire that crackled and echoed through the trees.

A second night in the car found Marty once again wide awake, staring out the front windshield at the darkened outline of the giant fir trees. The words that Gerry had read that morning echoed in his head, and the flying motorcycle faded. New thoughts of God out there in the distance, looking out for him, calmed the anxiety that had overwhelmed him the last few days.

The next morning, the pair read a few more chapters before they headed on a long hike through the spectacular mountain forest. Good-hearted neighbors brought by some food for their dented ice chest. That night they cooked hot dogs over a fire in their own camp.

As the sun faded and the fire died, they lay down on the top of the picnic table and marveled at the massive number of stars scattered across the night sky.

Gerry fell into a comforting silence, and Marty became lost in his own thoughts. He felt the tension releasing from his body. His eyelids grew heavy, but the beauty above riveted him back to attention. He didn't want to miss the display.

With no moon or city lights to mute its vibrant array, the sky mesmerized his mind and stimulated his senses. So dense were the stars that he couldn't make out even the most familiar constellations. He did, however, recognize his own smallness.

Am I really this insignificant? he thought. "In the universe's vastness, what difference does my life make?" He realized he had said this out loud and noticed Gerry was looking over at him.

"I could have died the other day. Twice. I could have died two different times and who would have cared?" His emotion was catching up with him. "I suppose my grandma would be sad, but what difference would it make in the grand scheme of things?"

After a few minutes of silence, Gerry spoke up. "There is another story we can read tomorrow. It's about this guy named Abraham. He was looking up at the stars like this and had an encounter with God."

"Why don't you tell me about it now," Marty said, assuming he was going to, anyway.

"Well, Abraham is this old guy who has been traveling around a lot, sort of like a nomad, living in a tent and herding sheep and goats. He is frustrated because he doesn't have any children to inherit his stuff." Gerry adjusted his back against the hard table. "So, the Lord tells Abraham to look up at the stars and try to count them. You can imagine the object lesson. Then God says, 'That is how many descendants you will have, Abraham.'

"The Bible says that Abraham believed God. He took Him at His word, and God said that that was all He wanted from Abraham."

Marty lay still and listened to Gerry tell this strange story.

"So, Abraham wasn't good or holy because he accumulated wealth or even because he always went where God told him to go. Abraham was good in God's eyes because he went from unbelief—you know, 'I'll never have kids'—to belief. He believed what God promised him, that he would have 'more descendants than there are stars in the night sky.' He dared to believe God, and that was all that God was looking for."

"That is kind of heavy, Gerry, but it sort of makes sense," Marty said. "Lots to think about."

When Marty returned home, he dug out the Bible he had put away in the back of his closet. He remembered thinking it was stupid when a teammate gave it to him, but he hadn't thrown it away. *More like hid it*, he thought as he began to read.

After that, he read a little each day.

The stories about Jesus particularly intrigued him. "Now there is a radical."

If this stuff is true, he thought, *then maybe life is making a little more sense.* He was no longer suffocating from the confinement of a low-lying ceiling that held no answers or comfort. He was gazing into the limitless sky of possibility and hope.

Four months later, Marty climbed out of his blue Dodge Demon and walked across the parking lot of Johnson Elementary School. He felt twelve again. How many times did he get called to the principal's office during his brief career as an elementary student? There were a few, and usually totally unjust.

He was twenty years old now and in the middle of his sophomore year in college. What could Mrs. Gould want to see him about? Had he mouthed off to someone? A parent complaint?

He wasn't planning to coach anymore. Two years in a row he had coached basketball teams that made it into the NorCal Tournament at the end of the season. It was a painful memory of the Hagginwood Hawks that lost in the finals last year. The reffing was terrible—all his best players fouled out by the end of the game. He never got over the distaste for the system. His team had worked hard, then got cheated out of the victory. Could someone from the tournament have a beef with him? His mind raced, trying to imagine what she wanted.

He pushed open the double doors that led into the building. As he walked down the hall, he remembered the last time he had been summoned to the principal's office. The same smell of fish sticks and apple sauce hung the air and took him back to Babcock Elementary, circa 1964.

There had been this new kid, bigger and meaner than most. Possibly because of the need to make himself known, he would wait for the end-of-recess whistle, then drop kick the red rubber ball as far out in the field as he could, sending some hapless fourth grader scurrying out to get it. He could never make it back in time and got in trouble for being late.

Marty had gotten so fed up with this new kid that one day he went up to him and pushed him to the ground yelling, "Knock it off, jerk!"

The usually inattentive playground-duty teacher saw Marty push the kid. She wasted no time and immediately sent them both to the principal's office.

Everyone at Babcock had lived in terror of the principal. He reportedly brandished an electric paddle that inflicted a shock along with a swat—precursor to the electric chair.

Not only was this terrifying, but the principal only had one arm. A one-armed hit man paid by their parents to keep them in line.

The boys appeared before the man, shaking in their Keds, and each told their side of the story. Turned out, he had no electric paddle—in fact, no paddle at all. He had sent Marty on his way with a warning and gave the new kid the "what for."

Marty snapped back to attention when the school secretary motioned, with a very low level of enthusiasm, to enter the principal's office. He found Mrs. Gould sitting at her desk, eyes squinting painfully behind thick, black-rimmed glasses.

"Marty!" she exclaimed, standing up out of her chair. "Thank you for coming."

Her obvious pleasure at seeing him put him at ease. Maybe he wasn't in trouble after all.

"Please have a seat." She motioned to a low-backed vinyl chair that faced her desk. Another identical chair sat empty next to him.

Obediently, he sat down. He watched the rather stout woman slip the black glasses up on top of her curly gray hair as she moved around her desk and sat down in the empty chair.

"I'll get to the point, Marty," she said with a gentle smile. "Our sixth-grade boys need a basketball coach." Marty let out an imperceptible sigh of relief, followed by a vague sense of irritation.

Of course they do, he thought, without letting on that these schools always needed a coach. With never enough money to hire a coach, they needed a volunteer.

She started in again. "You have an excellent reputation in the district. I am told that you are a wonderful coach with compassion and care for kids. Johnson has never had a team before. This school has all female teachers who don't know a thing about basketball. Our kids don't know a thing about it either, but I am convinced that some would like to learn."

Marty gazed out the window to observe the "playground" at Johnson Elementary. One eight-foot basket—chain net, rusted rim—at the edge of a cracked and pitted asphalt pad.

He listened to her carry on about the disadvantaged school. He thought about what it would take to get a team into shape. It motivated him when kids improved and learned to love the game. He was surprised at how short a time it took to get him excited about coaching again.

"We couldn't pay anything," he heard her say. "But your help would mean so much to us and the kids who want to play."

At this point, he hadn't said a word. His emotions had gone from fear, to suspicion, to a well-known rush of excitement.

He heard himself ask, "When is the first game?"

"Tomorrow," she answered.

Chapter 4

Arkansas, August 2002
Twenty-Five Years after the Murder

Detective Pete Willover arrived in Little Rock Arkansas' Adams Field, then rented a car for the drive over to Hot Springs. He saved a few bucks for the State of California by renting a compact with no AC. The forecast predicted ninety degrees, which wasn't bad compared to Sacramento in August. The slight miscalculation: the humidity.

Having spent all day cramped in two different flights, he was glad to drive to the small town of Hot Springs. Even though his shirt was soaked with sweat before he even got to the car, he looked forward to the solitude.

This case he was working on had haunted him for twenty-five years. The brutal murder of a fifteen-year-old kid had gone unsolved and had been shelved until the recent advancements in DNA testing. Solving this murder would bring a satisfaction he seldom experienced in his career as a detective.

When Pete arrived, he was welcomed by Sheriff Michaels, the head of the Hot Springs Police Department.

"I didn't get many details regarding your visit, Detective. What's the story?" the sheriff asked. "You are a long way from the

California sunshine."

"I'm part of a new cold case task force in Sacramento. I've been working on a homicide case from the seventies." Pete passed the case file to the sheriff, then shifted his weight, hoping for an invitation to sit down that never came.

"It's this Jennings character." Pete continued, as the sheriff scanned the file. "I liked him from the beginning for this murder. Now with the more advanced DNA tests we can, at the least, rule him out."

"Okay, you got your search warrant?" Sheriff Michaels asked.

"I'm good to go."

"Sounds like you have your bases covered, Detective. So, let's go rule him out." The sheriff picked up his keys and motioned to follow him to his car.

They drove fifteen minutes to the Jennings place. Surprised by the domestic scene they found, they paused a minute before getting out of the car. Two kids played in the weed-infested yard, a heavyset woman hung clothes on the line, and a vicious-looking pit bull tested the strength of his chain attached to a post on the porch. The barking beast looked as if he could pull the whole structure down if pressed.

The woman watched the men get out of the car and head to the front door. With heavy-lidded eyes and a bored expression, she went back to her work without a word.

The sheriff knocked on the door. "This is Sheriff Michaels. Can we come in?"

Pete fingered the warrant, folded neatly in one pocket, and the DNA swab kit in the other, hoping there wouldn't be trouble.

A gruff voice hollered from inside the cabin, "Yeah, come in."

As the two men entered, the man with the gruff voice asked, "What's going on?"

Pete was stunned to see the effects the years had made on Dean Jennings. The tall wiry kid was now heavy, disheveled, and completely gray. He sat, overfilling a wheelchair, with both legs amputated below the knees. Pinned-up pant legs covered two stumps dangling from the chair toward the floor.

"What the heck happened to you?" Pete asked without thinking. "I mean, the wheelchair?"

Jennings looked squarely at the detective. "How do I know you?" he asked, ignoring the man's insensitive question.

Pete recovered himself enough to look Jennings in the eye and reveal their past acquaintance. "I'm Pete Willover. I interviewed you back in seventy-seven in Sacramento."

Jennings's hazy gray eyes sharpened and revealed memory. "Oh yeah, that murder in Del Paso Heights. Yeah, I remember you. What are you doing out here?"

Pete pulled up a chair, sat in front of Jennings, and tried to get the guy's guard down a little. "I know it sounds crazy. I'm close to retirement so they have me with a different department now that closes old cases." He smiled and chuckled a little. "Let's just say they indulge me while I wait for my retirement."

Jennings nodded with indifference but said nothing.

"I just have a few questions, as you were the first on the scene back then," Pete said with as little concern as he could muster.

He continued in a nonthreatening manner to ask innocuous questions that he hoped would not arouse suspicion. They talked for a few minutes about Jennings's memory of the case, then Pete thanked him and stood to leave.

Pulling the kit from his pocket, he said, "Oh, one more thing. It would help to collect a DNA sample. It is just a Q-tip swab on the inside of your cheek. If you don't mind."

Jennings looked at him silently for a minute. Pete assumed he was weighing his options. Obviously, not knowing anything about DNA testing.

Jennings nodded and said, "Yeah, Okay."

A few minutes later, Michaels and Pete returned to the patrol car and pulled out of the gravel driveway back to the county road, glad to be away from the dismal scene.

"I may be a little dense, Detective. But how was that an effort to rule the guy out?" Michaels asked.

"Well, let's just say, if this sample rules him out, I will be very disappointed. But I am betting . . . it will not."

He attempted to explain that evidence from the original crime scene, preserved and stored away, would provide the proof needed to solve the murder. Proof that Pete could never get in 1977.

Five months later, Pete Willover returned to Arkansas from Sacramento, this time with an arrest warrant. He was not going to miss this bust.

The entire Hot Springs Police Department piled into every car available. With an arrest warrant, an aging homicide detective, and enough weapons to ensure capture, they headed out to Jennings's place. It was a little much for one guy with no legs, but they turned on the sirens and sped to the dilapidated cabin in the woods.

Chapter 5

Fifty-Six to Six
Sacramento, December 1974

Marty arrived at McClellan Elementary with his new team, the Johnson Jaguars. With a weighty sense of impending doom, they entered the school's gym, where the two teams would battle.

Marty knew the kids were nervous, but the fear seemed to worsen when they entered the gym. None of them had ever been in a real gym, let alone played basketball in one.

For Marty, the place evoked the familiar. The well-known sounds of sneakers skidding across the floor and multiple balls bouncing in a disorderly cadence.

He carried a mixed bag of thrills and disappointments into that gym. He had been a hero, but he had also been cut from more than one team. He received pats on the back and once got hit on the top of his head by the coach's clipboard. Athletics gave him confidence, scared him to death, challenged his abilities, and shaped his character. Athletics had the power to do all those things simultaneously.

He had coached a winning team in this league the year before, and this team, McClellan, had been their number one rival. Marty's old team, Hagginwood, had beaten McClellan, earning a spot in the Tournament of Champions at the end of the season. Now, the smug look on the coach's face sparked the memories of that last game. They came flooding in and threatened to force an abrupt retreat.

These are sixth graders, he reminded himself. *Kids that just want to play.*

Even though the stakes were low, and his pride tender, his competitive instincts were kicking in. He hoped to win at least one game this season, but he was pretty sure it wouldn't be this one. It was a tough spot for Johnson to draw McClellan for their first game. Teams had very good memories, and this team was motivated to beat Marty.

"Okay, guys," he called out after a few minutes of warm-ups. "Huddle up."

It had been painful to watch his dubious team warm up on the opposite end of the court from the home team. Opposite end of the court; opposite in every way from the McClellan team.

Flimsy white T-shirts for uniforms was the least of their problems, but it was the most indicative. These kids were on the losing end of the economic scale, talent scale, and every other scale you could think of. *This will be a slaughter*, he predicted.

Any hope of a showing vanished as soon as the game began. Four eight-minute quarters later proved the prediction. Although he had two kids that were five ten—Don Byers and David Ramon—they were slow and clumsy. Bobby Ruiz was fast and athletic but a goof-off and didn't know the game. If charm could have added points, Scott would have been the MVP. As it was, he wasn't much help. Mike was all heart and enthusiasm, but the youngest, shortest, and least athletic player.

McClellan's coach was relentless. He played his best players and held back nothing. His drive came from some other world as his team pummeled the Johnson Jaguars. Marty watched with arms folded and temper fuming. He was seeing red because of the overzealous coach, not because his team had stumbled up and down the court, overpowered by the boys in bright red-and-white uniforms that seemed to glisten under the fluorescent lights.

Marty didn't want his team to think he was frustrated with them. He knew he could look threatening to these kids that didn't know him from Adam, but that was the last thing he wanted. He made his best attempt to encourage the boys, but their enthusiasm drained as the game wore on, and Marty was afraid they would never want to play again.

Even Mike struggled to be positive. "What the heck? I get it, they are good, but what the heck?"

"All right, guys," Marty said at halftime. "We have some work to do over Christmas break, but hang in there for the rest of the game."

He attempted to explain how to guard the ball better and how to keep control as they captured rebounds and headed down court to their own basket. The problem was, they never got a rebound.

If they tried to dribble down court, the ball would inevitably bounce off the foot of the dribbler or get stolen. A McClellan player would scoop it up, then fast-break to his own basket. They knew how to make layups, something the Jags had yet to learn.

Every attempt at a basket flew wildly by the hoop and resulted in a rebound by McClellan. The shots that did make it were flukes. The worst part was the complete lack of teamwork. They had never played before, but they looked like five blind clowns running aimlessly around the court with shoes that were too big.

It was straight-up anger that swelled in Marty as he watched the McClellan team run up the score for no reason. As the fourth quarter started, the scoreboard clicked away. Each unanswered point felt like a dagger in the back.

Marty looked over at McClellan's coach and hollered, "Are you kidding?"

An audible sigh of relief came from the Jags and their coach when the final buzzer sounded. Marty forced himself to look at the scoreboard as his team left the court: 56 to 6. It couldn't have been more humiliating.

The McClellan team cheered and celebrated, having won their first game of the season. Marty couldn't help but notice the self-satisfied smirk on the face of the McClellan coach, communicating vindication.

"Don't worry, guys," Marty said without breaking eye contact with the rival coach. "We'll get another crack at them."

Scott looked at him like he was crazy. "You mean we have to play them again?"

At that point, Marty's desire for revenge outweighed his common sense. He knew the chances of ever playing this team again this season were slim, but his competitive nature kicked into gear with this kind of injustice.

"Maybe," he said. "Just maybe."

He directed the boys to the lineup of players for the traditional high fives, bringing even further humiliation as the McClellan team continued to gloat.

Marty took the team to A&W for root beer—hoping to lessen the sting. He wanted to keep things fun without letting on how determined he was to get back at the self-important McClellan coach.

It was Mike who had the first positive remark heard that day. "Don't worry guys. It will be okay."

The team looked at him in disbelief for a few seconds, then burst out laughing, relieving the tension.

"Oh, brother, what does 'okay' mean?" David Ramon asked.

Bobby piped in. "Yeah, what does that mean? That we won't die? That we will score eight points in the next game? That we will beat the pants off McClellan next time?"

They all cracked up, even the coach.

It took Mike's comment for Marty to realize that vengeance was not enough motivation. He needed to focus on these kids and help them stick to the program, see improvement, and have fun.

"Mike is right, guys," Marty said. "Don't worry. We have a

good idea now what we are up against as a team. We'll get better."

With their first game behind them, they piled into Marty's slight upgrade, a blue Dodge Demon and headed for home; dejected and embarrassed, but hopeful that maybe this guy could teach them how to play.

The first day of Christmas break, with the multipurpose room keys in his pocket, Marty decided to walk to practice, allowing some time to think. He had a few good drills in mind, but the team needed a lot of help. Getting used to handling the ball was on the top of the list and that list was getting longer by the minute.

He started to cross the street when he noticed a commotion near the outside wall of the school. Mike was easy to pick out of a crowd. He was about four and a half feet tall, if that. Three other boys surrounded him, pushing him around their circle with the flats of their hands.

"What a little pygmy," one of them said while the others laughed.

Another made a fist and pretended to punch Mike in the face then slugged him in the stomach instead. "Take that you little rat. You little pygmy rat!"

None of the boys noticed Marty coming toward them. "Hey! What do you think you're doing!" he yelled.

This time it was Marty towering over the kid who had landed the punch. He pushed the startled bully against the brick wall, grabbed him by the front of his shirt, and hoisted him up, leaving his feet dangling a foot off the ground.

Marty spoke with clenched teeth as close to the boy's face as he could. "If you ever touch that kid again, trust me, I'll make you regret it. Do you hear me?"

The kid couldn't speak, but the fear in his eyes and the slight nod confirmed that he heard and understood. Marty pulled the boy away from the wall and pushed his shaking body to the pavement. He hit the ground on his side, rolled over, jumped up to his feet, and ran like the wind to catch up with his friends who were long gone.

Marty held out a hand to help wide-eyed Mike get up. "Are you okay?"

Mike, white with fear and trembling like a boy who had narrowly escaped being beaten to a pulp, nodded. "Yeah, I think so."

"What was that all about?" Marty asked as they walked toward the multipurpose room for practice.

Mike shrugged. "My brother's friends. Potheads."

Marty opened the door, wondering what the rest of the story might be.

The term "ragtag" took on new meaning as practice got off to a rough start. Good news; two boys at five feet, ten inches tall. The rest was all bad news. No one could play basketball. Some were athletic, some were not at all. Some were fast, but the fast ones had attitude. They all had eyes that could roll to the back of their heads with impressive dexterity.

He started with the two boys who were the tallest. David and Don were both taller than any sixth graders Marty had ever coached, but neither knew how to play basketball.

David Ramon—dark, lean, and too cool—crossed the gym, looking for a chair to sit down on. With arms resting on his thighs, he waited for some proof that this team would be worth his time. The vagueness in his expression communicated apathy, but at least he'd showed up.

The other tall player was Don. If David was slow, Don was all but inert. His scruffy red hair and crooked nervous smile left one assuming he was not much of a threat. He had a slight edge on his teammate in the enthusiasm department, but it was not clear what he was enthusiastic about.

After some warm-ups on the court, Marty pulled Don and David aside with special instructions. "All right, guys. I want you both down at that basket." He pointed to the other end of the court and added, "I'll be there in a minute to show you what I want you to work on. The rest of you," he explained, "are going to work on layups and dribbling."

The other four looked at him as if he had just landed from outer space. The most potential lay with Bobby and Scott. They were fast, but doing nothing fast wasn't much better than doing nothing.

"We need more players," Marty heard himself say out loud.

His strategy, to focus on the basics, involved a simple drill: dribble-pass-dribble-shoot. He lined the boys up, showed them the drill, then headed to the other end of the court to give instructions to David and Don.

"Okay, all I want you to do," Marty said, "is stand on either side of the basket and shoot. Shoot-rebound-shoot. The point right now isn't to make a basket but to keep the ball in the air. Don't let it hit the ground."

He stood on one side and showed the technique of tossing the ball toward the backboard and catching it before it hit the ground. "Don't let your arms down but keep tossing the ball up like a volleyball."

The two nodded, not letting on that they had probably never played volleyball either.

"What do we do if we make it?" Don asked as he shot the foreign object toward the basket.

"For this drill, I just want you to keep shooting. Don't let your arms down, don't move around, just shoot-rebound-shoot. You can keep the ball high so the other team can't reach it. When you are rebounding, whether it is your shot or the other team's shot, you want to keep your arms up high and keep the ball up high. I want you to rebound your own shots and rebound your opponent's shots."

After a few minutes, he had just turned to go back to the others when the doors opened and in walked a kid dressed in a T-shirt, shorts, and baseball cap.

The newcomer met Marty at center court and with obvious apprehension.

"Hi, Coach."

Marty turned his attention to the new kid, hoping for a miracle; someone who could play. "Hi," he answered as he walked closer.

"I was wondering if I could go out for the team. Are you taking any more kids?"

"It depends," Marty said. "Are you going to wear that A's hat all the time?"

The newcomer looked confused for a second, then seemed to recognize Marty's Giants hat and laughed. "I don't know, Coach. Maybe I can convert you."

"Never," he said with a grin. "Are you a sixth grader at Johnson?" He dodged an errant ball that rolled to his feet from the other end of the court.

"Yep," was the hesitant answer.

"Well, we have already had one game, but we really could use more players. Why didn't you come out last week?"

"I didn't know that being an A's fan would be a problem, but I wasn't sure if girls could play."

Marty turned to face her, realizing for the first time that this newcomer was a girl.

"Well," he said, "I don't know. Do you know how to play?" Not that this had been a qualifier for anyone so far.

A big smile spread across her freckled face. "Yeah! I have a hoop in my yard and a bunch of brothers."

Marty scratched the back of his head. "Well, you can practice with us this week. I'll check with Principal Gould, but it should be okay."

No sooner had he spoken the last word, than she broke into a sprint and headed to the group of boys making their sad attempt at dribbling.

Marty hollered out after her, "What's your name?"

She grinned again. "Penny. My name is Penny and worth every cent!"

Marty watched in amazement as she entered in effortlessly. It took a few minutes for the guys to realize who she was and only a few more to know she could play better than any of them.

Encouraged that Penny fit in so well, he watched as she made her shots with ease and accuracy. Glancing back to the other end of the court, he saw Don and David remaining with steadfast obedience, under the hoop, tossing the ball up to the backboard.

"Coach," Don yelled. "This hurts! My arms are killing me!"

Marty ignored those moans and groans and turned his attention to the complaining coming from the other end of the court.

"This is so boring! When can we play a game?"

"Why is there a girl on the team?"

"Dribbling is boring, I just want to shoot."

"All right, knock it off. If you guys don't want to get crushed every game, then you need to learn some skills." He grabbed a ball as it bounced by. "And I'm sure you have noticed that Penny is the only one of you that knows how to play."

He reorganized the kids for the drill and started them up again.

"If you make five baskets in a row on this drill, you can take a break." He knew no one would make five baskets except maybe Penny, and she didn't want to take a break.

A few days later, Marty parked his Dodge Demon as close to the multipurpose room doors as he could get. He got out of the car and stepped gingerly on his tender sprained ankle. He winced with pain as he took a few steps and tried to loosen it up before practice started. Suddenly, some movement caught his attention from across the school's athletic field.

Squinting in the sunlight, he spotted Mike on the top of a chain-link fence. He was scrambling to get over as two older boys came up behind him. Mike jumped from the top of the fence, braced himself for the landing, and ran across the field. The two older boys stood at the fence and watched him run away until they spotted Marty eyeing them, then took off in the other direction.

Thankfully, he didn't have to run after them this time. "Were they bothering you again?" Marty asked when Mike finally slowed down and reached the safety of his coach.

"Nah, they told me they would pay me twenty bucks if I wouldn't tell on my brother anymore."

"Tell on him for what?" Marty asked as they walked together the last few painful steps toward the multipurpose room.

"I saw them smoking dope the other day and I told my mom." He took a breath and continued. "My mom works a bunch of jobs and isn't home much. My dad's not around, so I just thought for my brother's sake, she should know."

"Did you take the money?"

"No. I just don't want him to get into trouble like my dad. That's all. I don't want him to end up in jail or something."

Marty put his hand on Mike's shoulder. "That was a good decision, to not take the money."

Mike stopped and asked, "Coach, are you limping?"

"No big deal. Just a sprain from a game yesterday."

"Oh, sorry about that, Coach. Is this a bad time to talk to you about something else?"

"Naw, what's up?" Marty asked.

"Well, I was just wondering if maybe, I could be like a manager for the team? I could set up for practices, gather up balls, that kind of thing. I can yell and cheer with the best of them." He looked up and winced a little. "I can help in any way you need, Coach. I'm just not sure I will be much help on the court."

Marty smiled. "That is a great idea, Mike. Yes, for sure, it would help me out. I would love it and the team would, too. I can teach you to keep the stats."

Marty tossed him the keys. "Why don't you go unlock the door and find some balls for us."

Mike smiled and took off to help get practice started, yelling, "Thanks, Coach! I'm ready to hit the ball running!"

Marty watched him, unsure if he heard him right. Anyway, each player on the team was a challenge in the skills department, but Marty knew Mike was not only younger than the other kids but also not quite built for basketball.

Chapter 6

Sacramento, 2002
Twenty-Five Years after the Murder

The reporter sat opposite detective Pete Willover in the Pancake Parade on Folsom Boulevard. In truth, he was a college student getting info for a submission to the school newspaper. It didn't take long for the veteran detective to figure this out, but he didn't let on.

Pete mopped up his egg with the last of his pancakes. The young reporter watched with indignation, as he had already finished his bran muffin. Pete pushed aside the sticky breakfast plates and silverware and took a swig of coffee. The bus boy arrived, cleared the table, and came back with a fresh pot of coffee.

The bus boy, in an uncomfortable-looking white button-up shirt and white apron tied around his waist, poured the steaming coffee into Pete's mug but pulled back when the kid-reporter covered his mug with his hand.

With that, Pete leaned back in the red vinyl booth. "Now what is it exactly you want to know?"

The reporter stared at Pete with an air of superiority. "Are you going to drink more of that crummy coffee?"

"That's your question?" Pete raised his eyebrows and took another swig.

The reporter blinked and looked down at his notes. "Yeah, I'm trying to understand this DNA thing for an article I'm researching. It all sounds like *The Twilight Zone,* and I'd like to clear it up a little. You know, lend some credibility to the process for my readers."

Pete smiled, mildly offended by the third insult, not to mention the notion that this kid would give any credibility to anybody. "Okay, son. I'll try to help you out."

Over the pancakes and sausage, Pete had given the guy a little info about his background in law enforcement. He tried to be gracious and not demean the guy, but it was getting hard. Pete knew full well the only detective this kid had ever met was Andy Sipowicz, or maybe Lenny Briscoe.

"You know how fingerprints work, right?" he asked. "Everyone has a unique fingerprint, and the police have perfected the gathering and reading of fingerprint information. More like Sherlock Holmes than Rod Serling."

The reporter nodded, pen in hand. He stared at Pete with that look that junior reporters and know-it-all cops get when they are unimpressed.

"We all have unique DNA as well. You find it in blood, semen, saliva. You know, body fluids left at crime scenes." He took another sip of coffee. "I could take a Q-tip, swab the inside of your cheek, or yank a strand of hair from your head. I could then take it to the lab and get a test that would show me your unique DNA signature."

The reporter put down his pen, folded his hands in his lap, and continued to listen.

The kid's body language told Pete he better try to make this more interesting. "So, the DNA thing, as you call it, started with paternity testing. If you have the child's, mother's, and father's DNA, you can determine paternity or maternity. You can tell gender. You can tell if the sample is human or not. You can compare a sample to that of an offender to find a match. Lots of uses when it was first tested in labs."

The reporter leaned in. "You can learn that, and they can use it as evidence against someone in court?"

Pete, encouraged that the guy was paying attention, continued. "Well, not at first. The labs were not as sophisticated as they are now, so it wasn't 'good science.' There was a lot of work to do to get the process perfected so they could use it as solid evidence in court."

Pete offered more history of DNA. "It was 1987 here in California when a rapist, leaving DNA evidence on his victim, received a guilty verdict."

He added some cream and a few packets of sugar in an attempt to improve the coffee. "At first, there would be a pretrial motion to determine if the laboratories were reliable." Pete smiled. "You can imagine all the lawyer gymnastics to get tests thrown out before trial."

The reporter nodded and jotted something on his yellow pad.

"Anyway," Pete said, "the testing got better, and more evidence was holding up in court. Finally, the FBI came up with a computer program, CODIS, which stands for Combined DNA Index System. It brings together, in a happy partnership forensic science and computer technology."

The reporter, writing with intensity now, jotted this down. He looked up and asked, "Wait, Combined DNA Index System?"

"Yeah, kind of like the Library of Congress. They keep profiles of DNA samples from crime scenes and from known perps. The program finds matches. Cops from across the country can enter the data they have and hope for a match from the CODIS."

The reporter stared at Pete. "More like *The Matrix* than *The Twilight Zone*, huh?" He looked down at his notes. "So, what happened in the OJ case? Why didn't the DNA evidence hold up?"

A slight shadow passed over Pete's face. "Yeah, that was a fiasco. The defense convinced the jury that the police mishandled the evidence. High-powered lawyers with plenty of money won the day on that one." He shook his head and stared into the cup. "A real rotten deal."

The trial, publicized on TV and newspapers, and opined over for years, left Pete with a pain in the pit of his stomach. "Not to get too technical, but we list DNA profiles in local, state, or national data banks. CODIS can generate leads for us by getting a hit or a match with info we give and info they already have."

The reporter nodded. "And what if the DNA profile doesn't show up on CODIS?"

Pete took another drink of his now annoyingly lukewarm coffee, then held it up toward the nearest waitress. "Well, that presents a problem. If we are pretty sure about the offender, we get DNA from other means. We have to get creative, let's say."

The waitress in the white uniform and gold apron set a new mug down and poured from the silver carafe.

"And I should add," Pete went on, "that the Index gets bigger all the time. Millions of DNA profiles and counting."

The reporter continued to scratch down notes. He looked up at the ceiling for a second, thinking about his next question. "What do you mean by 'get creative'?"

Pete took a swallow of the hot coffee and shrugged.

The reporter stared at the career cop and seemed to realize he would not get much of an answer on that one. "So, can you tell me about any current cases that you are working with CODIS?"

"No," Pete said with conviction. "But I can tell you that the office I work in, created especially for cold cases, is busy. We only work on unsolved cases. But, with the help of DNA testing and indexing, we are working at closing as many as possible."

"What cases?"

"Well . . ." Pete cupped the piping-hot refill in his hands. "You will know when we solve them."

Chapter 7

Anger Management

The team worked out together every day over the Christmas break, running drills and practicing the basics. This was the first order of business. As the week wore on, Marty introduced a few simple plays. He made the most of Don and David's height, Bobby and Scott's speed, and Penny's skill.

Marty arrived at practice one day to find Don sitting on the curb outside the multipurpose room door, looking a little forlorn.

"How you are doing, Don?"

"Okay, Coach."

"You're here early. Even Mike hasn't shown up yet."

"Yeah, everyone at home took off for some football awards thing for my brother. I didn't have to go so I'm here."

"Let's get inside and get started." Marty unlocked the door and led the way to the equipment closet. Don helped him search for as many balls as they could find and tossed them out into the court.

They each grabbed a ball and planted themselves under the basket. The same drill: shooting, rebounding, and shooting again.

"Have you been on a team before, Don?" Marty asked.

"Not really, Coach," he answered. "My older brothers, all three of them, are on every team there is, though," he added without looking away from the basket. "I've tagged along to a lot of their games."

Marty nodded knowingly. "How is that for you, Don? Having brothers who are the center of attention."

Don was silent for a moment while he continued to toss the ball up against the backboard. "It's great," he said flatly. "They are the stars of every show, you know?"

Marty continued to rebound the ball, modeling the drill he had instilled in the two tall players. "Yeah, I think I do." The silence reflected what Marty knew was a painful reality.

He thought of his own younger brother, Les. Eager, talented, but always in the shadow of his older brother. Marty himself wasn't in anyone's shadow, but he knew what it was like to be invisible.

"I only have one brother, but my folks were always too absorbed in work to pay much attention to either of us. It's a drag, you know?"

Don kept his eyes on the ball, continuing to toss it up to the backboard. "With sports, my brothers are like robots: so intense and competitive. They are always being sworn at by screaming coaches, not to mention my dad always yelling from the stands. I can't stand to go to their games because of that. I'm glad you don't yell at us all the time, Coach, even though you would have good reason to."

"Oh, I get angry a lot, Don. I complain about refs, sports league officials, all of it can be maddening. But I hope with this team, we can get better and have fun too. I know you haven't played much, but we need your height. I can't teach height, but I can teach you to use your height to make rebounds and score from close in."

Marty caught the determination in Don's face as he concentrated on the drill. Rebounding the ball and shooting it back up to the hoop over and over. The reflective moment passed as the heavy metal door opened and rest of the team entered.

He called the kids in and instructed them to sit down on the floor. Maybe another pep talk would get them going. "Okay, guys, listen up. Your first game was a hard one. I know it wasn't pretty, but we had to start somewhere, and it told us a lot of things."

"Yeah," Ramon shouted, "that we suck!"

They all laughed and nodded their heads.

Bobby chimed in. "Also, that we stink!"

Before anyone could make another crack, Marty said, "Hold it, hold it. That isn't what I meant. We learned that we have some great assets."

"What did you say, Coach? We have great what?"

Bobby stood up, turned his back to the coach, and wiggled his rear. "Pretty great, huh?"

More laughter.

"Listen." Marty tried not to laugh. "We have speed, and we have height. There isn't another team in the league with our height. That will really help us on defense and offense. The speed of the rest of you is huge."

The team stared up at him, not sure how to respond. These kids didn't get compliments often, let alone declarations of advantage.

Marty smiled. "All right, I know that most of you have never played before, but you're learning. So, let's get at it today and get ready for our next game."

"Yes!" A yell went up from the little crowd sitting on the floor in the multipurpose room at Johnson Elementary. They clapped and cheered, while Marty privately swallowed his doubts.

Marty decided to change things up a little with a new drill. "Okay guys," he ordered. "Off with your shoes."

Moans and groans followed, as the team took off their shoes and left them on the baseline.

"Okay, run down to the other end of the court and wait for me there."

While they ran the length of the court, Marty rearranged the shoes in a pile to mix up the pairs.

He left the pile of shoes and went back to where the team waited for him. "When I blow the whistle, I want you to run to half-court, touch the center line and run back here." He paused, making sure they were all listening. Fortunately, the pile of shoes had their curiosity piqued.

"After you touch this baseline, run down to the pile of shoes and find one of your own." He looked at each player. "Got that? Only one shoe."

"Oh, man." It was David Ramon who made the first complaint. "This is going to be gross!"

"Ramon!" Marty snapped. "How about you demonstrate. Bring back your shoe, drop it here, run to the center line, touch it, back here, touch the baseline, run to get your other shoe. When you get back here, sit down, and put your shoes on. Got it!"

David rolled his eyes, but Marty was pretty sure he liked being called Ramon. He executed the drill, huffed and puffed while putting on his shoes, and then jumped to his feet.

"That was perfect, Ramon. Go put your shoes back in the pile, then come back here to lead the drill."

Mike stood next to Marty with hands on hips. "Wow, Coach. This could be the hump that broke the camel's back. It looks hard."

Marty looked at Mike with raised eyebrows. "What?"

"They might not want to play anymore," he said, assessing the team.

"Mike," Marty said. "It's 'the straw that broke the camel's back.' Don't ever say 'hump.'"

The clueless look on Mike's face said enough and Marty chose to not tease him or repeat his mixed-up idiom.

Conditioning was important to their game, but basic skills were essential. Learning to dribble and move, pivot, pass, and shoot all were things to work on every day.

The only outside shooter was Penny. Marty made every attempt to get the team to move the ball around, passing with ease and then eventually getting the ball to her. Scott was quick at layups and was improving, but still, the team had a long way to go.

As with every team he had ever coached, attitude made things challenging. Goofing off, whining, cockiness, not to mention establishing the proverbial pecking order. Sixth graders were notorious for it.

Marty watched this little team with a keen eye. He wanted them to have fun, but not waste their time. He wanted them to get better at basketball, but not think they were better than their teammates.

Marty moved around the court, helping the kids with dribbling and passing drills, when he noticed out of the corner of his eye, the outside door to the multipurpose room open slightly. Not wanting to interrupt the drill, he waited to see who was coming in.

A young kid stood inside the doorway bracing the door with his back, not moving into the building or going back out. Marty thought it might be Bobby's cousin Johnny, who Bobby talked excitedly about. Another player would be great. Marty had a good idea what the new kid was thinking. *Do I try something new and look like an idiot? This looks like fun but kind of lame too.* All thoughts Marty experienced as a kid himself.

The kid stood still in the doorway, chewing on his nails, watching the team, when suddenly Bobby came through the door behind him.

"Hey man," Bobby said with his usual enthusiasm. "You beat me here. Come meet Coach, he's cool."

Johnny folded his arms across his chest. "This looks boring."

"It's fun!" he said. "Coach is teaching us how to play. You would be great on the team. Come check it out."

"What about those two guys?" Johnny said, pointing to Don and David Ramon standing under the basket throwing the ball up repeatedly. "David is cool but that redhead is a dork."

Bobby laughed. "He's okay. Coach has those two guys by the basket because they are so tall. We are the only team with guys that tall. The rest of us are learning to dribble and pass and shoot. It's fun."

Marty, hearing their exchange, decided to go help Bobby with his recruit and walked over to the doorway.

Johnny looked unimpressed, but Bobby said, "Hey, Coach. This is my cousin Johnny. Can he join the team?"

"Hi, Johnny." Marty noticed that Johnny still held the door open with his back. "That would be great if you want to play."

"Come on, Johnny." Bobby didn't seem to mind learning something new, but Johnny appeared to not want to take the risk. "You'll be great! You're fast, man, and Coach will teach you the rest."

Johnny kept watching, his penetrating brown eyes staring out at the team. Suddenly he blurted out, "Are you kidding?"

"What?" Bobby asked, following his gaze.

Johnny turned back to Bobby. "A girl?"

"Yeah, that's Penny," Bobby said, in defense of his new friend. "She's the only one on the team that has ever played before."

"Listen, Johnny," Marty suggested. "Why don't you stay for practice today and then see if you want to be on the team. Like Bobby said, most of the team have never played before, so you'll be okay." He turned to the rest of the team and called them in to give instructions.

One hour later, Johnny, covered in sweat, tried not to appear too excited. Marty knew he was having fun, and he was fast. He noticed Johnny kept his eyes on Penny with frustration that he couldn't do all that she could. *Lots of attitude to work on, as well as skills.*

When practice was over, Coach stopped Johnny on his way out of the gym. "Johnny," he called out. "Hang back for a minute."

The others moved out of the gym, and Johnny, looking like he expected to be told to never come back, waited by the door.

Johnny watched Mike put the balls away in the equipment closet and turn out the lights.

He walked past Johnny and said, "See you later."

Johnny said nothing and stared at Mike as he walked away. "Man, that kid is a shrimp," Johnny said under his breath. He turned and saw Marty coming toward him. "Is that why you have him cleaning up?"

Marty pulled the keys out of his pocket and motioned for Johnny to step outside while he locked the door.

"Mike is an important part of the team." Marty looked Johnny in the eyes. "He is here every day, and he helps me a lot. So, Johnny, what do you think? Do you want to be a part of the team? You are fast, and I'd love to work with you to get good at guarding and shooting."

With a look of surprise, he said, "Yeah, cool. Uh, yeah thanks, Coach."

"Good," Marty said. "Be here tomorrow, same time, and be ready to work hard."

It was on the walk home that Johnny thought he might have made a mistake. A black '72 Chevy Monte Carlo drove up next to him and drove slowly up the street as Johnny continued to walk.

"Hey, man." The voice of his cousin Mano rang out from the driver-side window. "Where are you headed? Don't tell me you just came from Johnson!"

The three guys in the souped-up car chuckled.

Mano started in again. "You gonna play basketball?" he mocked with baby talk. "Gonna play with the little kids."

Johnny kept silent and continued up the street, his heart beating wildly. Only a block from home, he kept walking as if a dog was gnarling from behind a fence.

Mano was not ready to relent. "Why don't you screw those

babies and come ride with us. We've got weed, man, and you could make some money if you helped us sell it."

Johnny turned and looked at his high-school-age cousin, Mano. At that moment his car seemed like the scariest place on the planet.

He forced a reply. "You don't want me hanging around with you guys," he said finally, plucking up all the courage he had. "I don't think you want a baby back there in your cool ride."

Before they could reply, Johnny turned up an alley into the dark. The Monte Carlo stopped but was too far past the alley to follow him. He heard laughter coming from the car, then the distinctive sound of peeling tires.

Chapter 8

Sacramento, 2000
Twenty-Three Years after the Murder

"The name is Willover, sir. Detective Willover, Sac PD." Pete spoke into the phone he held between his chin and shoulder. He shuffled through a mound of files and papers on top of his small desk in the shoebox-sized office. "Yes, sir. That is right, I'm checking on the DNA analysis I sent to you." Finding the information he needed, he added, "Yes, file number one four three four dash seven eight."

He stared up at the ceiling while he listened to the Mamas and the Papas sing "California Dreamin'." The familiar hold feature of the state forensic lab telephone system made him want to punch something. He had five cold cases from the early seventies that he was working on from the new DNA analysis program, and it seemed like each one left him on hold with the lab for an inordinate amount of his day.

His transfer from the detective squad to the new cold case unit was not glamorous duty but a chance to readdress cases that distressed him and made him want to right some wrongs with new technology.

Pete had already dealt with the lab in this case. Extrapolated

DNA from a family member would help in matching the DNA on the evidence from the murder. Getting DNA from Jennings himself would help in court.

"Yes, I'm here," he said into the phone as he picked up a pen and scribbled down the information that came from the monotone lab tech on the other end of the line.

He had waited for months for the information, calling roughly twice a week with a vain notion that the guys over there at the lab would tire of answering the phone and hurry the test. Of course, they had no such notion, so here he was calling one more time.

Pete reached for the warrant application file and filled in the info so he could get authorization as soon as possible. If patience was any kind of virtue, he had developed it in spades on this case.

The murder had occurred almost twenty-three years ago. At the time of the original case, there had been no proof to arrest the suspect. No proof. They had put all the evidence from the crime scene in plastic bags slipped inside cardboard boxes, housed on a metal shelf in a cavernous evidence room. Thank God, Sacramento detectives had been meticulous in keeping evidence from unsolved murders.

Chapter 9

Fearless

To anyone else driving by on the freeway, it was a hospital like any other. For Penny it was frightening. Rising in the sky, the red brick structure filled Penny with dread. Light streamed through each window, penetrating the blackness. Floor after floor, each window revealing the untold drama in those rooms.

That was where they had all died. Every time she passed that building on the freeway, she sunk down in the back seat of her parents' beat-up station wagon and curled up in a ball.

All three brothers had died that night. She could not picture the car accident in her mind. She forced herself not to imagine it, but whenever they passed the hospital, she relived that middle-of-the-night race to the ER.

She remembered her mother's sobs, her father's white-knuckle grip on the steering wheel, and the rain. That icy rain that pelted them as they rushed from the parking lot, through the automatic doors that propelled them into the hellish place.

She remembered the feeling like it was yesterday. Her senses bombarded by bright lights, strange sights, and chaotic sounds. She would never forget all those frantic people shouting orders, machines beeping, and trays crashing to the floor.

Penny experienced things that night she shouldn't have. The waiting room reeked of alcohol and vomit. People were sprawled across vinyl chairs. Hushed voices and hurried footsteps all sounded like death, without a word spoken. Then the doors swung open to reveal a doctor in ER scrubs, with a green cap covering his head, and a face filled with agony. That was when they knew.

In contrast to the ER, the funeral had been eerily quiet. Flowers filled the church with a sweet odor meant to lessen their pain. The priest pronounced words of comfort—at least he tried to comfort with soft words and tender sentiments.

So, she spent hours in the backyard, shooting baskets. She shot with her brothers' ball into her brothers' hoop, practicing the things she had seen her brothers do. She could handle the ball as well as any boy at school. She could make shots from anywhere in the yard and execute fluid layups and free throws with near-perfect accuracy; and she dared to dream she would play on the team. It was a miracle they let her play.

With Christmas break over and the school week back to normal, the Johnson Jags played their second game. At first, it seemed predictable. Johnson started the game chasing Ben Ali players up and down the court. Even the jump ball, won by Ben Ali, sent the ball to the opposite end of the court. Marty took a mental note to work on Ramon's jump ball tip.

The good news, Ben Ali was a terrible team. If bets had been taken on the outcome, it would have been a toss-up. Their apathetic coach, who never stood up, checked his watch and shook his head at the scene.

Marty kept looking over at the door, waiting for Penny. The others had ridden over with him, but no sign of Penny. She would make a difference, but where was she?

He yelled for a time-out after about five minutes of play. "Okay, guys. Our best strategy right now is to keep control of the ball. This team isn't fast or aggressive, so you can take your time. Johnny, you take the ball down the court. Don and Ramon, get down court and stand on either side of the basket. The rest of you, pass the ball around then either to Don or Ramon, whoever is open." Marty looked at his two tall guys. "Then you guys take your shots. Okay?"

They stared at him, as if waiting for a magic wand to appear and enable them to do the things he asked.

The ref tossed the ball to Bobby on the sideline, who threw it to his cousin Johnny, who took off down the court toward Johnson's basket. Marty grimaced when he noticed Johnny tense up with nerves. Fortunately, the ref wasn't calling traveling or double dribbles today.

Johnny got down the court but pulled back, looking for someone to take the hot potato. Scott motioned from across the court to receive the pass. Johnny dribbled in place, spotted Ramon under the basket, and passed it to him.

Shouts from the sidelines pleaded. "Shoot, shoot!"

But Ramon looked at his teammates wide eyed, for someone else to take the responsibility. Rather than going in for a short shot off the backboard like he had practiced a million times, he froze. The whistle blew. Too much time in the key.

At halftime, the score stood at a solid zero to zero. Marty weighed his options. *What do I correct? What do I encourage?*

The Ben Ali coach called in his players and told them to "Listen up."

But they didn't appear to do so. Two kids jabbed each other, laughing. Another bent down to tie his shoe. Another bounced a ball absently, while yet another waved to his friends who were watching.

Marty got down on one knee and looked his players, who sat trying to catch their breath. "You guys are giving them a run for their money," he said. "Now listen. What's missing right now is confidence. Don't be afraid of that basket. You're dribbling well, passing all around, but don't be afraid to shoot. You've made those shots, all of you. If you miss, that is okay, you can try again. But if you never take a shot, that score will stay the same." He pointed up to the scoreboard to make his point. "Fearless, you guys. Fearless!"

They all looked at each other and repeated the admonition. Tentative at first, then loud and in unison. "Fearless!"

Back out on the court, the game returned to its slow, unsure pace.

Get your bearings, Marty said to himself, hoping the team would remember his words.

Johnny took the ball down the court and passed to Scott, then Scott passed to Bobby. Bobby pivoted and, with two shaking hands, pushed the ball upward toward the basket.

It missed. Missed completely, but it seemed to break the spell. Somehow, the rebound found its way to Don, who passed it back to Ramon, who remained unguarded under the basket. His shot went up, bounced off the backboard, and landed in the hoop.

The team clapped with enthusiasm. Johnson was in the lead, two to nothing. Smiles as broad as the Sacramento River spread over the faces of the team as they raced down the court to set up their defense.

The tension built with every possession, knowing every basket was a game changer, every trip down the court, terrifying. The 2–0 score changed to 2–2, then 4–2, then answered with 4–4. It didn't take long for Marty to realize he wasn't breathing.

The sound of the gym door opening drew his attention and surprise as Penny darted into the room, tears streaming down her face. She ran over to Marty, out of breath and red-faced.

"I'm sorry, Coach. My mom needed me today and wouldn't let me leave. When I got everything done, I rode my bike as fast as I could. I'm so sorry."

"It's okay, Penny." He assured her. "Wait, you rode your bike over here?"

She nodded, wiping the tears from her eyes.

"Wow! Okay, go sign in with the ref."

With two minutes left on the clock, Marty called a time-out. "Okay, guys." He took a breath, trying to calm himself. "Two minutes left. Get the ball to Penny." He patted her on the shoulder. "If you get the ball to her, she will know exactly what to do."

Penny beamed with pride. Johnny rolled his eyes.

"One more thing," Marty added. "Whatever you do, don't let them score. Remember what we practiced on defense." The huddle broke. The team went out on the court, and the race was on.

Bobby dribbled to the basket then passed to Johnny, who ignored the coach's instructions and threw a brick that bounced wildly off the rim directly into the hands of a Ben Ali player.

He turned, dribbled down the court, and made a similar shot as Johnny. Bobby caught the rebound, and with seconds left, moved up court with a game face that Marty hadn't seen before. He faked a pass to heavily guarded Ramon—*where did he learn that?*—then made a quick, crisp pass to Penny, who had been invisible up to that point.

She caught the pass, pivoted, and made a clean shot—a thing of beauty. The shot sent the team into hysteria, just in time for the whistle that ended the game.

After congratulating Ben Ali for the great game, then tossing Penny's spray-painted gold Schwinn in the trunk, the tribe of banshees piled into Marty's blue Dodge Demon and hung out the windows squealing, "Fearless," all the way to A&W. They yelled out the car windows with crazed excitement, like twelve-year-olds who had just won their first game ever. Usual attempts at being cool and not caring about the team vanished.

Marty understood they were beside themselves, but he also was pretty sure it could be the only game they would win. With that in mind, he had promised ice cream in the root beer for the win.

The team went inside, ordered the promised root beer floats, and squeezed in together at a table. They chattered, recounting the entire game, celebrating each minute of the mighty victory.

Out of the corner of his eye, Marty noticed a guy moving toward their table. The closer he got, the wider Marty's eyes grew with recognition. Larry Jinks, the meanest kid from his high school.

Six feet of pure intimidating muscle, a bushy unibrow drawn together in a perpetual scowl, not to mention the menacing effect that filled the air. He wore a tight black T-shirt with bold white letters that said, "Who's Next?"

"Hey, Brown." He sauntered up to the table.

"Hey, Larry. It's been a while."

"I would have killed you, you know," he said, not wasting any words on pleasantries.

"Yeah, I know, Larry." Marty didn't take his eyes off the guy, nor did any of the kids at the table.

"They saved your butt. You know that, Brown?" He growled.

Living in a tough neighborhood, the kids knew a thug when they saw one. Their jaws went slack as they braced for a fight.

Marty worked to change the subject. "I hear you're boxing professionally now. That's cool."

Jinks blinked and softened his stance. "Yeah, that's right. I'm a pro. You can't even imagine what I would do to you now," he mocked smugly. His sneer didn't go unnoticed as he walked out the door.

The team looked at Marty, as if they weren't sure whether to laugh or go hide.

Bobby piped up. "Okay, Coach. What's the story with that guy?"

Marty didn't dare turn around to follow the blast from the past. "Is he gone?" he asked quietly, then took a drink of root beer.

Johnny kept his eye on the parking lot and the stranger. "He's getting into his truck. Ford 'Highboy.' Black. A beauty," he said with admiration.

The engine roared and the tires screeched out of the parking lot, like an exclamation point.

All eyes shifted back to Marty, who was taking a deep breath.

"Well, it started when I was a sophomore in high school. I had just moved in with my grandma on Santiago Street. She was kind of old and my parents wanted me to help her out. Not protect her so much as make it look like someone else was around."

They nodded knowingly.

"It's a kind of rough neighborhood, you know. When I first moved in, like the first day, I was cutting through the alley to get over to Raley's for the five-cent ice-cream cones."

"Those were far out. I wish they still had those," Don said.

"So, I'm walking across the field to El Camino, and I see this kid getting pushed around by a group of older kids. They wanted his money or something. They're cussing and shoving the kid around. So I yelled from across the field, 'Hey, leave him alone!' They didn't pay any attention to me until I got closer and yelled again.

"Well, as you can guess, they turned their attention to me. The kid ran away, and they started yelling at me, 'Who are you, punk?' Stuff like that."

Marty raked his fingers though his hair. "They turned their attention on me, the white guy, and I knew I was in trouble. 'Who do you think you are?' followed by a shove that sent me flying. I got up quick, but unfortunately, they weren't through. The biggest guy slugged me in the stomach, my knees buckled, and I fell to the ground. Man, it took everything I had to not throw up."

Marty took a sip of root beer then went on. "So, the big kid says, 'Next time, mind your own business, punk.' Another shove sent me flying again, but they walked away and left me alone."

The team had all put down their floats, completely engrossed in the story.

Don piped up. "Was that Larry guy one of them?"

"No." Marty laughed. "I'll get to Larry in a minute. It crossed my mind that I better learn to defend myself. But I didn't want to think about it."

The team stared at him in disbelief. Marty knew what they were thinking. How did someone as big as Marty become a target?

"Anyway," he continued, "that spring in PE, we had boxing."

Their eyes grew bigger still as they listened to him.

"Our PE teacher was kind of thickheaded but very passionate about boxing. First, we put on gloves, hoping to look like we knew what we were doing. Of course, we didn't. But he taught us stuff like how to stand at an angle to make our bodies a smaller target. He taught us to distribute our weight across both legs for balance, and to shuffle our feet and stay moving. But he would holler at us nonstop, all red-faced and mean. 'Hold your right glove up by your cheek and your left out in front a little.' He showed us this stuff while dancing around, trying to look like Ali. It was funny, because he was fifty years old and had a good paunch.

"He also loved to use me as a guinea pig. He would throw punches to unguarded body parts to show the proper techniques. Every time I went to PE, I was nervous. I knew I would get thrashed."

This time Penny spoke up. "Why were you his guinea pig, Coach?"

"Maybe because I was tall, or I always looked terrified," he reflected. "Well, he was also the head football coach. He had great running backs, all-state in fact, but no line. He hassled me all the time, but I didn't want to play. So he tormented me in PE. I guess he thought if he could make my life miserable enough, I'd be willing to beef up his offensive line."

Marty's attention went back to that PE class in 1970. "He had us spread out all over the gym, practicing the step-drag footwork and how to pivot. The pivot helped us make defensive moves and attack at the same time. Because I played basketball, I could do the moves naturally.

"It wasn't so bad when we were just messing around in the gym.

Especially when the coach picked kids other than me to entertain himself. But then, one day, he announced he was setting up a tournament." Marty paused for effect and heard the groans and watched the nervous looks.

"I hated it. I could see the need to defend myself against thugs and bullies, but to hit my friends in the face. Not fun at all. I was always dreaming up ways to get out of PE. Take a fall, break a bone, run away from home. You name it, I thought about it. But anyway, I won all the bouts in the tournament, at least the ones in my class."

"There was more than one class?" Bobby asked.

"Oh, yes. There were two classes. Two kids ended up in the final bracket. I was the winner in my class and the other was—" Marty motioned toward the door. "—Larry Jinks."

The team groaned again.

"Larry had not only won his bracket. He had knocked out two kids."

"Knocked them out?" Penny asked in astonishment.

"Yep, he knocked two kids out cold. They got dragged off the gym floor. Our meathead PE teacher dragged them out of the gym by their ankles!" He shook his head at the memory.

"Man, I was so scared. My last bout was Friday and the bout with Larry was on Monday during PE."

"Did you spend the weekend practicing? Did you practice on your little brother?" Don asked, probably knowing that would have been his role had any of his brothers faced the likes of Larry Jinks.

"Ha. No. I was so scared I could hardly breathe. All I did was worry. I stayed inside all weekend and filed through all my strategies to get out of school. I knew I was no match for Larry. You saw him! He is huge. He might be a pro now, but he was skilled in high school." Marty looked down at his root beer, reflecting on a time he hadn't thought about for a while.

"Not only was Larry big and strong, but he was also mean as heck. He took drugs, he drank a lot, and always put on the tough-guy act, but it wasn't an act. A junkyard dog, if you get my drift," Marty said.

Don jumped in, "Like 'Bad, Bad Leroy Brown'?"

"That's right. My theory was that the whole point of the boxing unit was to watch Larry Jinks knock kids out. I was going to get killed. I couldn't imagine what it would feel like. The kid that hit me in the stomach that summer was no Larry Jinks, and it hurt like crazy."

There was silence for a minute as each kid appeared to process this information. Coach Marty, terrified? It probably seemed impossible. And yet they had just met the terrifying figure that had tormented him. They waited with bated breath for the outcome.

"So what happened? Did he crush you?" Johnny asked, looking like he was trying to be cool, but desperate to know. "Is that why you seem to have a little brain damage?"

They all laughed.

"Oh, wait," Ramon said. "Is that what happened to your nose?" Referring to Marty's obvious crooked nose.

"Very funny," Marty said. "I'll tell you that story another time. Anyway, I went to school on Monday with a dread I'd never known before. I kept thinking, now what do I do? Which foot goes where? Which fist does what? I was in a panic.

"Then my friend Gerry comes up to me in third period and says, 'Hey, Brown. Did you hear the bout got canceled?'

"I'm, like, stunned. What? Canceled? Could this be the miracle I'd hoped for? Then Gerry says, 'Yeah. The PTA got wind of the tournament and made the principal cancel the bout. All the knockouts. Moms aren't into that sort of thing. You lucked out. The PTA saved your butt.'"

"Oh man," Scott said, letting out his breath. "What did Jinks do? Did he want to fight you after school?"

"There was talk of that," Marty said. "But I'm pretty sure he knew the principal was onto him, so he stayed under the radar until he graduated. I guess he knew he had bigger fish to fry."

Mike piped up, "He obviously never forgot about you, Coach. I'd steer clear of him if I were you."

"What about the guy who punched you, Coach?" Penny asked. "Did you ever see him again?"

"Well, so happens that, yeah, I saw him again the next summer. I took the same shortcut one day, and he comes up to me all tough. 'Hey, honkey, give me your money, or I'll flatten you again.'"

They were all, once again, holding their breath.

"I said, 'No.' He said, 'What, honkey? What did you say to me?' I said, '*No*, man. I said no.' Then he hit me with his fist right on my jaw. Oh, man, it hurt like mad. I stumbled back, but thankfully this time I didn't fall." Marty couldn't help but smile at the memory. "I let him have it with a left jab he didn't see coming, right to his nose."

The group let out a cheer.

"Who's next?" Don said. "Right coach?"

"The guy is standing there wiping blood from his nose, kind of dazed. He can't believe it. He finally staggered off. Never saw him again. But I got to tell you, my hand hurt for like a week after that."

A few days later, Bobby asked Coach Marty if he had a hand pump for the basketball he found at home, buried in a box in the garage. "I've been practicing at the school hoop in the mornings, but my ball is flat."

Marty answered, "Sure Bobby. I've got one in the equipment closet. Can I ask why you are practicing in the mornings?"

Bobby explained, "The older kids in the neighborhood like our hoop here because it is an eight-footer, you know? They can dunk on it, so they hog the hoop all afternoon."

Marty nodded. "Right, that is a drag. Good job practicing on your own."

Bobby smiled and kept talking. "Yeah, I concentrate on the

back of the rim like you always say." He attempted a two-handed shot from the top of the key that didn't go very far.

"That is great, Bobby. I like your form. Let me show you the power part from your legs." Marty grabbed the ball and stood next to Bobby, demonstrating what to do with his feet.

"Remember to put your right foot a little ahead of the left, but keep your feet apart for a broad base of support, and it will give you better balance. Now bend your knees and use the momentum for power when you straighten up." Marty moved up and down, bending his knees and moving up to shoot the ball. "Does that make sense?" he asked.

Bobbie tried to keep his feet in the position Coach suggested and bend at the knees. "That's right, Bobby. Keep working on that movement. If you do that enough times, you'll develop muscle memory, and you won't have to think about it."

After a few tries Marty added, "The key, like I said in the Ben Ali game, is to not be afraid to shoot. You'll never score if you don't ever shoot."

Bobby continued to shoot the ball. "It is easy in practice, Coach. But in a game, I get flustered and just want to pass the ball away."

Marty nodded with a knowing smile. "Yeah, it is hard to take your shot with arms waving all around you." He picked up a ball off the gym floor. "Here, take this ball home with you."

Bobby looked puzzled. "Why do I need a second ball?"

"When you're practicing, bounce the second ball in front of you, then shoot around it like this." He showed him by bouncing the ball high in front of his feet, then shooting the other ball with a little jump to get around the first ball.

"Cool," Bobby said as he watched the shot go into the hoop.

"Don't lose that ball," Marty warned. "It belongs to the school."

Chapter 10

Sacramento, 1999
Twenty-Two Years after the Murder

Tracking down Jennings was proving to be difficult. Pete's need to get a sample of his DNA in order to match it with the evidence saved from 1977 was now the pressing issue. A little digging revealed that Jennings had married in 1986. Pete, after an exhaustive search, miraculously found the ex with her new name in Stockton.

A few months before, he had stood at her door, fifty miles away from the murder scene, and tried to explain his idea. "I am sorry, ma'am, to dredge up these old memories," he'd said. "But there are new ways to test evidence, and it might help our investigation if we had anything to test that belonged to him."

She stared at him, expressionless, from behind the screen door. "Something that belonged to him? What are you going to do with it? ESP or something? Like a psychic reading? I think that's a lot of bull."

"Yes, ma'am. I agree. No, this is a scientific examination. Do you have that would have hair or skin cells or something?" He shifted his weight uncomfortably, knowing he sounded like a crazy person.

"Yeah, that's a joke. That jerk never gave me anything except grief," she said in disgust. "I really don't want to talk about him. My daughter will be home from school soon and I've never told her much about her dad." She stepped back evasively and moved to shut the door.

"Wait," Pete said. "Wait, you had a child with him?"

She paused and replied, "Yes, she's thirteen. She was born after he left. Or, I should say, after I kicked him out. I'm remarried now to a decent guy who loves Kimie like she was his own." Her anger dissipated to gratefulness.

Pete cleared his throat and spoke quickly before she changed her mood. "She could help us, ma'am. It would help our investigation if we could get samples of both your DNA."

She looked at him quizzically. "How do you do that?"

"I need a swab from the inside of your cheek with a Q-tip." He tried to smile to convey the simplicity of it, but knew it probably sounded like nonsense.

"How do I explain that to her? Let alone my husband," she asked. "I don't want them to know anything about that time of my life."

"I understand completely," he encouraged. "I have what I need to get the samples."

He thought for a moment. "If they ask, you could tell them it's for a census thing. Testing for the effects of vaccinations or something like that?" He smiled again, trying to seem as trustworthy as possible.

After an awkward minute, she reached for the handle on the screen door and let him in.

Chapter 11

Shuttle Play

Scott walked tentatively up the walkway after pausing a moment to decide if he should go inside. His home was an unpredictable place, and he prided himself on the ability to sense trouble. Truth was, there was always trouble. There could be no one there, or they could all be there. Maybe they would all be there screaming and throwing things. Best-case scenario, Dad passed out on the couch without the usual blaring TV or annoying old records stuck and repeating their sad lyrics over and over.

It was January, and the winter air stung Scott's sweaty body. Practice had been brutal but somehow invigorating. He had never run so much in his entire life. The short walk home left him shivering. He opened the screen door to find the front door ajar. He walked into a stone-cold, empty living room in its usual disarray.

His first inclination was to go to his room and close the door, but he was starving. He headed to the dark kitchen, flipped on a light, opened the fridge, and foraged. After grabbing the package of bologna with one piece left, he gave it a sniff. The near-empty jar of mayo would help soften the usual stale bread.

The white bag with colorful dots lay crumpled on the counter. He reached in and found a hard heal at the bottom. He pulled it out, slathered on the mayo, slapped on the bologna, and folded up the concoction. Taking a bite, he looked around for something else.

Empty beer cans littered the counter. Everything else—chicken noodle soup, a couple of eggs—would require cooking, and he was not about to put out that kind of effort.

He was leaning over, checking a bottom cupboard of the narrow galley kitchen for some cookies or chips, when a noise startled him to attention.

"Where the heck have you been?" came the familiar slurred inquiry from his dad.

His father stood filling the doorway to the little kitchen, all six feet, five inches of him. A quick glance at his dad's disheveled hair and dirty, wrinkled work clothes, confirmed he was drunk and dangerous.

"Practice, Dad. Basketball practice," Scott said, instinctively moving further away from the volatile head of the household.

"Basketball?" His dad sniffed. "That's a joke."

Scott breathed a sigh of relief as his dad staggered to the couch and flopped down. He was out cold by the time Scott stole past him on his way to his room.

Sitting on the edge of his unmade bed, he devoured the sandwich and weighed his options. His older sisters were out. His dad was working the night shift so wouldn't be leaving until ten. TV was not an option. It didn't cross his mind to do homework or clean up his room.

He pulled the sweaty T-shirt over his head and threw it in a pile of other rank clothes that had been accumulating. He dug a yellow "Bananas" sweatshirt out of the drawer and pulled it on over his head. His favorite. Dirty jeans would have to do, because that was all he had. He felt the slight ache of overworked muscles in his arms. *Cool,* he thought.

He pushed up his sleeves, opened the window, climbed out,

dropped to the grass below, and disappeared into the graying late afternoon.

First stop was the video arcade. No money to play, but the best place to find his friends. Even though he was a sixth grader, he liked to hang out with older kids.

The basketball team was the exception. He loved to play basketball on an actual team. In his own mind, he was easily the best player. He relished the fact that he was the fastest kid on the team. Even though he didn't shoot around much at school, the coach was adding new drills, and he was getting better.

His sandy blond hair and glassy blue eyes were his best asset out here in the streets. He had that "California surfer dude" look, to help him out if he needed it.

Scott often regretted that he didn't have his dad's height, but was thankful he didn't have his dad's abrasive, innate ability to tick off everyone he ever met.

Looking around, he spotted a group of eighth graders near the front door of the arcade. They were laughing at something known only to them. Scott scoped the scene to figure out what or who was so funny. It always paid to be aware of what made someone look stupid. He saw Martha something-or-other and guessed it was most likely her. She always dressed kind of weird and carried a load of books everywhere.

The one kid he knew, Terry, looked up and gave him a slight nod of recognition.

It always annoyed Scott that fourteen-year-olds talked to twelve-year-olds like they were seven, but he was glad for the greeting.

"How's it going?" Scott asked casually as he joined the group, assuming they were heading into the arcade.

"We're just leaving. We scored some weed from my brother, and we are going down to the levy to smoke it." Terry motioned for Scott to join.

Terry was one of the cooler guys in the group. His long scraggly hair and casual manner, emulated by the other boys, was the trademark for cool. Terry always took the lead on who got included and who didn't.

"Sweet," Scott said as indifferently as he could. No one would have guessed, but he was nervous about looking inexperienced. He assumed the older boys smoked pot all the time, but Scott had only watched.

They headed down the street, cut through an open field, and crossed Del Paso Boulevard. The streetlights were coming on as they turned up the path that edged the empty cement drainage ditch that the kids called the "levy." It wasn't really a levy, but that sounded cooler, like "American Pie" kind of cool.

They chose a secluded draw of low shrubs to sit behind and wrapped a few papers filled with cheap marijuana. It was easy to pawn it off to naive teenagers who mostly only pretended to be high.

A twinge of guilt sparked in the back of Scott's brain. Not from the illegality of it, but because he watched his dad get drunk every day. It made him stupid and mean at the same time. His dad was a jerk and a loser, he reasoned. Scott buried the feeling and took the joint as it was being passed around.

He watched the other boys as they took drags. At his turn, he was careful to hold it between his thumb and forefinger. He took a drag, attempting to not cough like a little kid. It was a show, but necessary. This was what it took to keep from being alone at night in his room, listening to broken records.

Scott related easily to the group as they talked about sports. Norte Del Rio High School football was over for the season, but the basketball season was underway. Scott didn't let on that Johnson Elementary had a team this year. There had never been a team at his school, and everyone would laugh at the idea. He hoped they would never find out.

"Did you guys see the game last Friday?" Scott asked nonchalantly. "Incredible. Lassiter was unstoppable. He had thirty points, man. Thirty points."

"I missed it," Terry admitted. "But I heard about it. Everyone was talking about it. Should be an amazing season."

Scott had overheard his sister's friends talking about the team. They were on the cheer squad and hung around the players.

"I'm thinking Grant will be the hardest team to beat. They have all their players back from last year."

Terry added his opinion. "Yeah, Smith and Evers are seniors this year and will kill it. Norte doesn't have anyone close to those two."

Scott agreed. "You're right, but Lassiter is good. If he is half as good at basketball as he is at football, they could do all right."

The chatter continued as the boys wrapped another joint and passed it around. Scott felt his status go up as he talked about stuff most sixth graders knew nothing about. He felt like a stock car inching its way from the back of the pack, passing one car at a time.

He lay back into the weeds and stared up at the emerging stars sprinkled across the clear January sky. He felt very grown up. Here in this place with these friends. They talked about things that made him laugh, shared crass jokes, and made fun of others who were weirdos.

As the banter quieted down, his thoughts wandered to Christmas. What a disaster. No money, no special food, no gifts, no mom.

He zoned out from the voices of the crowd and thought about the team. He loved that the coach let him run. He was sure he was the only one who loved running. Flying from one end of the gym to other, touching the floor with each turn, shoes screeching, outrunning everyone.

It made him feel good. At the gym, and out here under the stars, no one knew what a loser his dad was. No one knew the desperate pain he felt after losing his mom.

His thoughts drifted to the smiling, laughing face of his mother. She had died a few years before, riding on the back of a Harley with some guy they didn't know. Some drunk, dumb guy, who skidded into a cement embankment on some stupid road that led to nowhere.

She left Scott with two older sisters who were as lost and alone as he was. His dad had proven himself completely incapable of taking care of three kids, let alone coping with the loss of his beautiful, unfaithful wife.

Scott had never stopped picturing her on that bike, blond hair flowing, laughing, arms wrapped around the waist of someone she thought would bring her a few moments of freedom. His imagination never let him see the wreck. Instead, he remembered her that way, wind in her face, broad smile, free.

Walking to practice became a sort of pre-practice ritual for Marty. He enjoyed the time to make the mental transition from student to teacher. As he turned the corner onto Grove Street, he spotted Don ahead of him by a half block. He recognized his tall, stooped frame, short reddish-blond hair, and his ever-present brown, slightly flat basketball. He was moving at his usual slow lumbering pace toward the school, bouncing the ball against the pavement. Marty made a mental note to pull out the pump again.

Out of the corner of his eye, he saw Ramon crossing the street in front of him. Marty stopped and held back, hoping the two would bond or something.

"Hey, retard! Where are you going?" he heard Ramon shout to his teammate.

Don shouted back, "None of your business, meathead."

Ramon, equal in height, opposite in coloring, social status, and grade point average, picked up speed. "Wait up! Are you going to practice?" he asked.

Don continued to bounce the ball. "Practice isn't until four.

I'm going to shoot around while I wait."

"Mind if I shoot with you?" Ramon asked.

"Okay, sure. Come on. Maybe there won't be any older kids hogging the baskets."

"Can you say, 'fat chance'?"

Don laughed. "I know. It gets old. Today are tryouts for the eighth graders for baseball, so maybe they won't be anyone else here."

Ramon looked over at Don. "Wow, inside info. How do you know that?"

"Older brothers," he said.

Ramon nodded. "Hey, sorry for the crack, earlier. It has been fun to work together on the boards. You know, how coach taught us."

"Yeah, it is fun. I think we are even making some shots." Don bounced the ball ahead of him so Ramon could catch it and bounce it back.

Ramon laughed. "Far out, man. Do you come early a lot to practice?"

"Sometimes, I wait over there." He pointed to the picnic tables. "If everyone leaves, I kill the hour before coach gets here by shooting around."

"That's cool. I've been walking all the way home, watching TV for half an hour, then walking back. I'll come shoot with you if that's okay. My mom won't like me missing *General Hospital* though."

Don looked at him with curiosity. "Are you kidding?"

"No, I'm not. It is kind of tradition. It's okay. She'll catch me up."

Marty slipped out of sight near the multipurpose room but couldn't help eavesdropping on the conversation.

As the two five-foot-nine sixth graders approached the empty court, Don asked, "Want to play H-O-R-S-E?"

"What's H-O-R-S-E?" Ramon asked.

Don bounced the ball a few times. "I'll show you. I've watched my brothers. They don't let me play with them, but I think it's a simple game."

As the boys started taking their first shots, Ramon asked, "How do you think Penny knows all this stuff? She is such a great shot. I know she has older brothers too, but I can't imagine they let her play with them."

Don stopped shooting and held the ball. "Don't you know about her brothers?"

"Know what?" Ramon asked.

"She has five brothers, but three were killed in a car accident a few years ago. They got run off the road by a drunk driver. They all died."

"Oh, man," Ramon said, looking down at his feet. "I didn't know. That's got to be the worst thing I've ever heard."

"No kidding," Don said, taking another shot, trying for the third time from the same spot. "The good news, I guess, is that no one uses the hoop in the backyard."

"Sheez," Ramon exclaimed. "I may hate my brothers, but I wouldn't wish that on them."

Don chased after the ball that hit the rim and went flying. "I know. All my parents' attention would be on me to be the family sports hero. I'm kind of happy staying under the radar, if you know what I mean."

Ramon caught his pass and added, "Yeah, I know exactly what you mean."

Marty slipped inside the door unnoticed and satisfied that at least, Don and Ramon were becoming unlikely friends.

Later at practice, Marty gathered the team. "All right, guys!" Marty hollered as he attempted to get them under control. "Huddle up, we're going to learn a new play."

"New play?" Don said with a smirk. "I didn't know we knew

any plays."

Marty glanced over at Don. "Exactly."

As the team gathered, he started his explanation of the shuffle play.

He moved five players to strategic places on one half of the court. He only had six players, so they would have to learn this play without the aid of a defense.

"Johnny and Bobby will always be the guys bringing the ball down. The two of you," he explained to Penny and Scott, "spread out on the left and right of the key, with Don here at the right upper corner of the key. This play involves everyone who is on the court. You are all handling the ball, passing, moving, shuffling."

Once they were positioned, Marty showed them how to pass the ball, and rotate and cut, while keeping spaced across the floor. It was a madhouse to start, but he was diligent to stop and start them over and over, showing them the offense.

"Keep your head up, Johnny!" Marty instructed. "Dribble with your head up so you can see where you are going."

As Johnny moved down the court, head up, eyes scanning, Marty said, "That's right. Now start with a pass to Bobby. Don, pop out to the corner and wait for a pass from Bobby. Ramon, same thing on the other side. Bobby, you cut to the basket for a return pass and scoring opportunity."

They followed his instructions in slow motion. They all seemed to feel the impossibility of this, but Marty didn't let them stop to think. He just kept them moving.

"Important to remember, guys," Marty said, "you can only stay in the key for three seconds. One-Mississippi, two-Mississippi, three-Mississippi. That is why you keep moving, try to get open, but move."

Marty ran the play over and over. At first, the kids were so confused it was funny. They were laughing and cutting up.

"Come on, Coach," Johnny complained. "This is ridiculous. It makes no sense!"

Marty answered back, "It might not make sense now. But trust me, it makes perfect sense once you get the hang of it."

Starting over from the beginning, Marty shouted out the directions as the team tried to remember the moves. Like dance partners trying to follow in their minds what they had learned, they moved with slow caution. Their driving motivation? Don't look like an idiot while trying to remember the pattern.

Marty grabbed the ball and started over for the tenth time. "Remember when you learned to ride a bike?" he asked. "Do you remember how hard it was? Riding a bike! What could be simpler, right?"

Johnny looked over at his cousin with a smirk. "You should have seen Bobby. It was hysterical." He laughed again and shook his head.

"Yeah, we were all hopeless," Marty said with a grin. "But didn't you fall a million times, get back up a million times and keep trying?" They stared at him as the example began to make sense. "You all learned, didn't you?" They nodded and pumped their fists and gave each other high fives. "Okay, so let's do this drill a million times, mess it up a million times, and eventually, if we don't give up"—he paused for effect,—"we'll score."

He divided up the players, brought Mike in, and tried to simulate defensive players. The order they had developed turned into more chaos. Johnny and Scott just wanted to score, and their motivation switched from learning the play to showing off.

"Hold it." Marty entered the middle of the court. "Let's work on this without trying to score. I want you to learn to pass the ball, keep it moving, shuffle around the court with the pattern I showed you."

He motioned for the kids to get into their original positions. "The defense is there so you learn to run the play under pressure. It is still the same pattern, so let's try it again."

Marty walked over to the sideline and started the drill again, just as Principal Gould came in.

"Hi, Marty," she said with a smile. "How are things going in here?"

"Oh, hi." Marty backed up to stand next to her by the big double doors to the multipurpose room. "I think things are going great."

She stared out at the team and watched as the drill disintegrated into a disorganized mess. "Really?" she asked, a bit puzzled.

Marty shrugged. "Well, it doesn't look like much. But they're learning, working together, and enjoying it." He paused, then added, "I think."

She stood with arms folded across her chest and watched. She had no idea the team had reorganized itself and tried the drill again, without Marty's help. "If you say so, Coach," she said, shaking her head and turning to leave the gym. At last glance she stopped. "Wait. Is that Penny Parker out there?"

Marty took a gulp, realizing he had never run it by the principal. "Yeah, that's her. Turns out she is the best player on the team," Marty said matter-of-factly.

Mrs. Gould looked at him again. "Well, I would say things are going really well, Marty. Thank you so much."

The gym at Sacramento State College was humming. Fans filed in, climbed the bleachers, and geared up for the pregame show. The Hornets had never drawn this big of a crowd before. Today a few players from the San Francisco 49ers football team had agreed to play a charity game with a group of city Parks and Recreation employees.

That was how Marty entered the gym, lining up for drills before the action started. His boss, from his part-time summer job with the city parks, had asked him to play. He knew no one was watching him or cared that he was about to humiliate himself. No one except the small group of screaming sixth graders halfway up the bleachers.

Somehow, the team had found out he was playing in the exhibition game. They got someone to drive them to campus and pay for tickets. He suspected Principal Gould, but wasn't sure.

Les, Marty's younger brother, a shorter, equally athletic version of himself, stood in front of him, waiting for the ball. Marty peered up into the bleachers, hearing not only the team yelling his name, but his grandmother yelling as well. He hadn't noticed that Les had stopped and kneeled to tie his shoe. Marty ran right into the back of him, knocking them both to the floor. It was only the beginning of the indignity he would endure that day.

The crowd saw everything because the celebrity football players hadn't entered the gym yet. When they jogged onto the court, the crowd cheered with enthusiasm while the city employees took deep, anxious breaths.

"Remember, guys," Marty encouraged, "this is for charity."

They looked at him doubtfully. The only eight people in the entire city Parks and Rec Department with the courage to come out to play.

Marty watched as the football players warmed up. "They are huge," he heard himself say out loud. In particular, he spotted Willie Harper. A bulked-up defensive linebacker recently drafted from Indiana. Marty had followed many of the players on the 49ers since he was a kid. The players who showed up for the event were mostly defensive players, and massive.

Warming up before the game would be critical. Two weeks previously, Marty had an existential moment, a beautiful thing. He felt like he was flying when he ran down the court, jumped with perfect timing, and made a clean slam dunk. The first for him in an actual game.

Although Marty was tall, with long arms, his short fingers made dunking difficult because he couldn't palm the ball. He'd spent weeks doing lunges and lower-body weight training to gain some spring. He could finally dunk. Then came that fateful day when he tried it in a game.

He went up with perfect control, just the right touch and turn of the wrist. Then jammed the ball cleanly through the net.

It was his landing that failed. He landed on the foot of an opposing player, then fell to the ground in wrenching pain as his ankle twisted under his weight. Without a second to enjoy the shot, he felt searing pain shooting through his leg and foot. The game ended, then his teammates helped him off the court, and drove him to the ER.

Two different docs stated emphatically, "Stay off the foot. No basketball for the rest of the season."

Marty protested. "But the 49ers game is in two weeks."

"Sorry, son. No basketball for a while. No sports at all for the next couple of months" was the grim reply.

Marty had hobbled out of the hospital, barely making it to Gerry's truck without screaming.

"Sorry, man," Gerry said with genuine sympathy. "That 49ers game was going to be a slaughter with you. I can't imagine how it will go without you."

Marty looked over at his friend and wanted, not for the first time, to slug him. Fortunately for Gerry, he didn't have the strength to do it.

It was a few days later, on campus, that Marty, juggling crutches, books and shooting pain, ran into a friend from chemistry class. Marty told him about the injury as he leaned against the crutches, wincing.

Bemoaning the loss of playing in the charity event, he said, "It sucks, man. It hurts like crazy. They don't put enough aspirin in those little bottles to make a dent."

His friend Mark looked down at the swollen ankle that sported a lone flip-flop. "Hey, I have an uncle who used to be a trainer for the Dallas Cowboys. He specializes in getting players with injuries fit to play. Let's go see him and see what he thinks." He looked at his watch and added, "He's coming to our place for dinner tonight. How about if I pick you up and take you to meet him?"

"Really?" Marty asked. "Are you sure he won't mind?"

Mark shrugged. "Nah. He's kind of a showoff. He will love the attention."

Mark's uncle confirmed his nephew's prediction. He seemed to love being the authority in the room. "It isn't so bad, Marty. I'd say, throw out the crutches. You have to start walking on it."

"Walking on it?" Marty asked. "The doctor said to wait two weeks to walk on it."

"Well, yeah, that is standard treatment from docs who know nothing about athletic injuries." He continued to poke and maneuver the ankle. "You should ice it as much as you can in the meantime," he added.

"Ice?" Marty again asked incredulously. "The doctor said heat. He said soak it in hot water."

Mark's uncle laughed again. "Well, the newest treatment for this is intermittent ice and some heat. Gets the blood flowing to the injured area and reduces swelling. If you can get the swelling to go down, you will reduce the pain as well." He looked up and smiled. "Trust me on this. Come over to my place on game day and I'll tape it up for you. It will be tighter than a drum. Believe me, but you'll play like a pro."

So, the morning of the game, Mark's uncle worked his magic and wrapped it so tight that it felt like a new ankle. Marty walked on it gingerly, then normally, and now in the warm-ups he was forgetting about it.

Les stood to receive the warm-up pass. Without turning around, he murmured slowly to no one in particular, "We are going to get killed."

The first minutes of the game were completely one-sided. The football players were in town for several public relations events and didn't bother to practice for the game. The city employees had never played together until this moment. The only advantage, Marty thought, was that they were younger and maybe a little more agile. There was actually no advantage.

Four minutes into the game, the score was zero to ten. Marty realized quickly that their team had no agility at all. Already winded, the city team unanimously regretted the decision to play.

"Whose idea was this?" more than one player complained.

Les and Marty had played ball together their whole lives, and when they got in sync, magic happened. Marty scored the first basket, which inspired the rest of the team. Not because they wanted to win; they simply didn't want to look like complete losers.

As the buzzer sounded, ending the first quarter, the team plopped down on the bench. Sweat flowed, inadequately replaced by little paper cups of water.

The score stood at 8–30, 49ers. The good news: Marty was the only one who scored for the city employees. He knew it was crazy, but he was on fire. He didn't have much lateral motion with the ankle, but he could move forward okay, and the pain was manageable.

Les was passing the ball with brilliance, but the screens were good only if the football players weren't paying attention. The 49ers scored at will but couldn't figure out how to stop the only player on the opposing team that could shoot.

When the football players got a little more aggressive, they used their considerable girth to prevent the screens.

Players went down hard, over and over, until Marty finally said to his teammates, "Don't bother to set screens."

He could hear his grandma screaming from the stands, "Come on, Ref! Call something!"

He knew they weren't going to call anything. This was too much fun, watching celebrities mess with the city workers.

Without the screens, he started shooting further and further away from the basket. He landed crazy shots with supernatural accuracy. Even so, the scoreboard said 38–80. It felt useless and glorious at the same time.

Finally, with only the fourth quarter left in the game, the 49ers called for a reset of the scoreboard. It was a "charity" game, after all. Back to zero to zero, the score ran up to 16–30 with the bulk of the Sacramento City Parks and Recreation Department points coming from the injured Coach Marty.

As for the Johnson team in the stands, they were beside themselves. They all cheered for their coach like it was the US against Russia in the Olympics. For every shot, they stood and jumped and screamed and cheered. The folks in the stands were more entertained by those sixth graders than the celebrities on the court.

Marty, with his head down, could barely breathe, and felt the increased throbbing in his ankle.

Les came up beside him. "Marty, go sit out for a while." He leaned down toward his exhausted brother.

"I'm okay."

There was no way he was going to take a rest. The screaming sixth graders in the stands were motivating him to finish the game. *Thank You, Jesus,* he said to himself as he jogged back out onto the court.

In the end, it was a predictable loss, but Marty had scored an impressive thirty points and prevented total humiliation for his team.

The football players drew the crowd and the charity got the purse, but Marty won a new respect of his players on the Johnson Jaguars. When the game was over, the team couldn't contain themselves. They poured out of the stands onto the court and tackled their coach with high fives and wild cheers.

"We would take you to A&W if we had any money!" Bobby said excitedly. "But no ice cream because you didn't win."

They all laughed and headed out for their now traditional, post-game root beer—on the coach.

Chapter 12

Who's Next?

The team once again piled into Marty's car, this time to Natomas Elementary School.

When the door slammed shut, Don piped up, "Hey, Coach. *Who's next?*"

Everyone started to laugh, and Penny said, "We should have black T-shirts made!"

"Yeah!" Don added. "With a unibrow painted on!" They were riled up and bouncing off the walls. Marty wondered if the energy would help or hurt.

"Lame car, Coach!" ribbed one twelve-year-old after another.

"Not as lame as having to walk," Marty answered with a grin. "You know you love this car. Come on, admit it!"

"So lame," they all said, laughing and pounding the seat.

When the jeering died down, Don said, "Hey, Coach! I got a driving quiz for you. You ready?"

Marty grinned. "Yeah, I'm ready. Lay it on me."

"You are driving in a car at a constant speed. On your left side is a drop-off. The ground is twenty inches below the level you are traveling on. On your right side is a fire engine traveling at the same speed as you. In front of you is a galloping horse which is the same size as your car, and you cannot overtake it. Behind you is a galloping zebra. Both the horse and zebra are also traveling at the same speed as you. How do you safely get out of this highly dangerous situation?"

"I give up, Don. What do I do?" Marty said as he took the ramp off the freeway.

"You're drunk—get off the merry-go-round!"

Despite themselves, they all laughed out loud.

Even Johnny laughed. "That is a good one."

After a quiet minute, Bobby chimed in from the back seat. "Hey, you guys, did you see Jabbar last night? Wow, he is so hot right now. He had like fifteen rebounds."

When the whoops and hollers settled, it was Penny who voiced a quiet opinion. "Maravich is my favorite. But he plays for the Jazz now. They're a new team and not doing so good."

The car got silent. They all knew she was the best player, but probably never figured she would know so much about basketball.

"My mom likes me to watch sports on TV with her," she said in explanation.

When they reached Natomas, they scrambled out of the car and headed to the gym. They busted through the double doors to find a near-empty building. A few guys stood at one end of the court, shooting, and the Johnson team stood looking around, not sure what to do.

"Okay guys, warm-ups!" Marty shouted from the sideline and watched as they formed two lines in the backcourt.

They started the drill by dribbling the ball up to the basket. After attempting a shot, they passed to another player and ran back to the end of the line. Ramon grabbed the pass but stopped short, causing Bobby to run into him. They both tumbled on the floor, with the entire team laughing.

"Look, Coach!" Don said. "We learned this warm-up watching you and your brother in the 49ers game. Watch, we'll do it again!"

"Hilarious. How about some game faces, all right? Game faces!" Marty had to laugh and wondered how many times they had to practice that.

Eventually, the coach showed up, with his team straggling in after him. Once again, the underestimated Jaguars seemed not to be a threat.

The Jags huddled around, hands piled on top of each other, and shouted their new break, "Who's next!"

A few minutes later, the ref blew the whistle and tossed the tip-off ball into the air. Ramon, the tallest player on the court, didn't get the ball to a Johnson teammate. Natomas got the ball and headed for their basket.

Slow moving and inaccurate shooting kept the score low for the first few minutes of the game. Johnson slowed down as well and adapted to the pace. Johnny's steady hand kept control of the ball, and the team could set up the plays Marty had taught them in practice.

It was Don who attempted the first screen the team had ever tried. Don ran Marty's instructions through his head and moved to the center of the key to screen one of the Natomas players, but failed to plant his feet, causing him to run into the Natomas player with enough force to knock him down. The ref's whistle blew, charging Don with a foul. On the next possession, Marty called a time-out and motioned his team to the sideline.

As the team huddled up, Marty said, "Don, that was great. You had the right idea to set a screen for Scott. That is the exact idea. You just have to remember to plant your feet. You can't be moving. Does that make sense?" He looked at Don and the rest of the team.

"Yeah, Coach, I get it. Plant my feet, so I don't knock the poor guy out, right? No pulling a Larry Jinks on him!"

Marty laughed and knew his brightest, biggest player got the idea.

The next time the ball headed for the Johnson basket, Don

raised his hand to signal Ramon, planted his feet, crossed his arms, and waited for Ramon to pass to Scott. He ran straight at Don, then moved past him, leaving his Natomas defender blocked by Don.

The boys nodded enthusiastically, excited to have executed the play. They tried the play again, and Don scored once off his own screen.

"Yes, way to deliver!" Marty shouted from the sideline.

Mike sat right next to Coach Marty, keeping the stats and cheering for the team. "Go Jags," he shouted. "Defense, you guys, defense!"

Finally, Marty called for Penny. "Okay, Penny. They won't be expecting you to score. Let's show them what you're made of."

Marty overheard Scott say to Mike, "I've never heard of a girl playing basketball before. Do you think she can do it?"

Mike looked at him with a blank expression. "None of us have ever played before."

Scott shrugged. "Right."

Well into the first quarter, Penny went in. She ran the length of the court a few times, getting her rhythm. She was always open, because the Cougars were not sure how or if they should defend a girl. The vague assumption was that she was just giving "flying Scott" a break.

The trick for Penny was to convince Johnny to pass her the ball. He didn't. He looked all around the court for an open man but didn't seem to think about Penny.

At one turnover, Johnny took the ball out at the sideline and heard his coach's familiar admonition. "Penny is always open, dude."

With the score stalled at 10–8 Jags, Johnny must have known he had nothing to lose. He bounce-passed the ball to wide-open Penny, who stood on the very inside of the key, halfway to the basket. A simple one-handed shot hit nothing but net. A new sensation, that woosh of the ball through the net, gave them all a thrill.

During the halftime chat, Marty, down on one knee, encouraged the team. "Don, your screen was perfect. You were amazing. My only suggestion," he said as he looked at each player, "the point of the screen is to get open and score. Scott, you had the ball and Don blocked your defender for a second, but he was on you right away. Remember, if Don is open, pass him the ball while the defender is off guard. Make sense?"

Perfecting the screen and a couple more hoops from Penny, along with a little trust from her team, put Johnson ahead, 16 to 10 when the final whistle blew.

It was an embarrassment. Gerry's rusty '62 Ford pickup looked like he had swiped it from a salvage yard. Sad to say, it was their only form of transportation for the night. Marty's car was sitting in the driveway with barely a drop of gas after taking the kids home from A&W that afternoon. Gerry drove, while their friend Greg sat in the front. Marty, mulling over the game and making plans to improve the team, sat in the truck bed. It stunk of fertilizer from Gerry's last load, but they didn't have far to go to get to the theater. *Young Frankenstein* would be a welcome distraction.

With gritted teeth, Marty flopped from side to side with every bump in the road. A thirty-mph turn onto Bellevue threw Marty across the width of the bed, slamming him into the side of the truck. He could hear the guys in the cab laughing.

"Slow down!" he shouted as he rubbed the inevitable bruise that was forming on his thigh.

Movement from a driveway caught his attention. Marty looked over to spot a shirtless man swinging what looked like a belt. He could hear the man swearing at a little kid who was screaming and writhing in the hard dirt.

Instinctively, Marty stood up, stepped on the edge of the truck bed with one foot and leaped to the ground, then landed on his side in the street. He rolled, gained control, and jumped up to his feet to find himself face to face with the man wielding the belt. Marty pushed the man with both hands, sending him to the ground. Gerry, Greg, and the pickup kept moving down the street, not noticing the loss of their passenger.

"Hey!" he yelled, heart pounding. "What do you think you're doing?"

Stunned, the shirtless man shot back, "Who are you?"

"It doesn't matter who I am—leave that kid alone."

Marty smelled alcohol and recognized the glazed look of the man who stumbled slightly but turned his drunken fury on the stranger who had come out of nowhere.

Out of the corner of his eye, Marty saw the belt swinging around and heading straight for him. He caught it in one hand before it hit him, yanked it out of the drunk's hand, then swung it around and threw it over the neighbor's fence.

Meanwhile, the kid sat on the ground, looking terrified. When Marty reached out to help him, he winced, then moved away. Any thought Marty might have had of overstepping his bounds disappeared when he saw the tear-stained face and discolored welts on the kid's arms.

As the kid scrambled away to safety, Marty turned to the guy in the driveway. He moved in on his grimy, unshaven face and said with as much malice as he could muster, "Never hit that kid again, hear me?"

Walking back to the street, he spotted Gerry and Greg running toward him.

"Are you crazy? What were you doing?"

"It made me mad! He hit that kid with a belt!" Marty said, wide-eyed and shaking. "I guess it was instinct. I knew I had to get that belt away from him."

The three walked back to the truck. Gerry shook his head, "How do you know it wasn't his own kid?"

"I'm pretty sure it was. It's infuriating when people meant to be protectors treat kids like that. It isn't right."

Heart still racing and hands shaking, he looked back to see if the guy was following him. The drunk was standing still, staring in disbelief at the stranger who had just tossed his belt over the fence.

Marty sat in the theater with his friends, sulking over the stupid display he'd made on the way over. He felt justified, but stupid at the same time. *What gets into me?* His thoughts drifted to an experience in high school that seemed to color much of his motivation.

He had been desperate to make the basketball team. He had the skill, the height, the competitive edge, but back then the steadfast rule was that each player had to run a six-minute mile to qualify for the team. Because of severe allergies, Marty's mile, despite several tries, never made the six-minute time.

He begged the coach to let him try one more time on a rainy day, figuring the dry grasses and pollen would be lessened by the rain. The problem was that the dirt track was muddy. He gave it his best shot, but the stubborn coach would not budge on the five-second shortfall, so Marty never made the team.

It was humiliating and unjust. There was no one to advocate for him or even help him to work through it. Said and done. No basketball in high school.

Maybe that is why he was so driven to protect kids. No one ever protected him or spoke up for him when he was in trouble. Maybe that was the appeal of his growing faith in God. Someone who was there for him. *Maybe I just need to stop jumping out of moving trucks,* he thought as the movie started.

Chapter 13

Sacramento, 1998
Twenty-One Years after the Murder

Pete opened the newspaper and searched for the announcement that was to appear in the *Sacramento Bee* that morning. Finally, page six of section D. Not buried but not front-page news either.

> ### COLD CASE UNIT FORMED
>
> Sacramento County Police Department spokesman, Janet Hensman, announced the formation of a Homicide Cold Case Unit at the behest of Sacramento County Deputy District Attorney, Mary Schubert. Hensman reported that the new unit would be investigating crimes that were committed before DNA testing became mainstream. Experienced homicide detectives and part-time employees will man the new unit, charged with the task of reviewing hundreds of cold cases from the seventies through the nineties.

Pete, gratified about the announcement of the new unit, was motivated to get going on investigations that had been closed and filed as unsolved. Twenty-five years of cases that seemed to have been forgotten would now see the light of day. In the forefront of his mind was that Del Paso Heights case from 1977. That was where he wanted to start.

Chapter 14

Bust off the Bench

Marty pulled up the heavy garage door and was immediately hit by a blast of musty air. He walked into the garage and, with a frown, eyed the stacks of mismatched cardboard boxes, loose tools, and plastic garbage cans filled with unidentifiable odds and ends.

This is one garage that will probably never house a car, he thought to himself. He imagined these were things that hadn't made the cut when Grandma moved into the house a few years before. A divorced grandmother with a lot of stuff that she couldn't throw out but didn't want to have to look at all the time.

Marty yanked the chain that dangled from the bulb in the ceiling, stepped back, and was confronted with more boxes than he had imagined.

Grandma had asked him to find a box that contained picture albums. None of the cardboard towers had labels, of course. Marty pictured his grandma finding random boxes from the backs of grocery stores, then stuffing them with her belongings while furious over the latest antics of Prosper Brown, her mysterious ex. No one knew much about the guy, but he must have been something else to motivate Grandma to pack up and move across the country to get away from him.

Marty moved boxes, judged their weight, and made a stab at the contents. He was sure she didn't have a stash of books, but the albums would weigh about that much. Setting aside the light boxes, he dove into the ones that felt about the right weight.

He thought back to the day he moved over here from his childhood home a few miles away. That was a bigger house but filled with tension and stress. Moving in with Grandma, meant to be a protection for her in this rough neighborhood, felt more like a protection for him. He had been glad to move away from his distant, angry dad to a place of peace. If only there was a way to eliminate *Lawrence Welk* on Saturday nights, it would be perfect.

He pulled out a pocketknife, cut away the masking tape, and dug into the first box. A disappointing discovery of technical manuals from the place where she worked. He attempted to wrap the box back up and moved on to the next disappointing box of personal papers, legal documents, and years of tax returns.

After about four boxes full of junk, Marty found a small box wrapped haphazardly. It looked older than the rest and sparked his interest. It couldn't be the photo albums, but like a kid left alone with presents under the tree, he couldn't help himself. He took his pocketknife to the tape and pried it open. Crunched up newspaper filled the box and Marty pulled it all out, piece by piece, to reveal another small wooden box buried in the newspaper.

He took it out and examined the intricate carvings on the box that depicted a low sloping field of wheat swaying in the wind. The small metal latch swung open easily as he lifted the lid to reveal the contents.

At first, he thought it might be her old wedding ring. It turned out to be a huge solitary diamond sitting on a black velvet cloth. The diamond glowed in the stuffy dark garage, and he thought maybe it was more of a hiding place, rather than storage.

"It belonged to my father-in-law," he heard his grandmother say from the door of the garage.

Marty turned and looked at her, not sure what to say. "Sorry, Grandma, my curiosity got the better of me."

She was in her late sixties, not more than five feet tall. She never missed an appointment at the beauty parlor, keeping her hair blueish gray and tightly permed.

She walked up to him, barely reaching his armpit, her presence always comforting and confrontational at the same time.

"It's okay. You just better not tell anyone you saw it."

She grabbed the wooden box and gazed at the diamond—poised to tell the story.

"My ex-husband's dad was a bit of a . . . well, let's say he was not a good guy. He had a temper that was notorious. In fact, he was a Grand Wizard."

Marty wasn't sure he heard her right. "A what?"

"You know, a Grand Wizard. The Klan," she said, without emotion, while she gazed at the gem.

"You mean the Ku Klux Klan?" Marty asked incredulously. "In Indiana?"

"You bet. Back in the day. He ended up in prison more than once for his antics. The family pretended he didn't exist most of the time. Anyway, when I married your grandfather, everyone disapproved. Mostly because he had a similar propensity to violence of the alcohol-induced nature. Prosper's dad approached me one day and told me he was sure his son would be a louse. This stone, a family jewel, might come in handy for me someday. It is the only nice thing he ever did for me."

She gazed at the dazzling diamond. "Most men think a woman can't make it on her own in this world. I guess he figured I would end up desperate and alone." She took a breath. "Well, he was right. I was alone, but not desperate."

Marty looked at his grandmother with admiration as she went on with her story. "I have always assumed he stole it. That might have been the actual reason he gave it to me, so I've never had the courage to sell it." She continued to stare at the gleaming thing. "I couldn't put it in a setting and wear it, for obvious reasons."

Marty thought about his dad's temper. He was always so ticked off about everything. *I guess he comes by it honestly*, he thought, then realized his own temper was an issue more times than not.

Breaking the silence, he said, "Grandma, maybe a safe deposit box would be good. If anyone broke into this garage, they might find it like I did."

She looked up at him. "Smart boy. That is a good idea, but I need your word that you won't tell anyone about this. Especially your dad. This could be a temptation beyond his ability to ignore."

Marty smiled. "Yeah, sure. I never saw it, Grandma, but I still can't find the picture albums," he said nonchalantly as he looked around the hopeless stack of boxes. Hesitating for a moment, Marty plucked up the courage to ask, "Are you ever lonely, Grandma? I mean, moving across the country, living alone?"

Looking up at her grandson with pride, she smiled. "Well, I miss my brothers and sisters. They warned me about Prosper, but I was stubborn." She laughed a cynical little laugh. "But, I have you now, don't I?"

She walked away, out of the musty garage, into the light of the warm Sacramento sun. "I'm not lonely at all," she said, looking back over her shoulder as she headed back to the house.

The drive to the next game took the team into an unfamiliar neighborhood. The manicured lawns, gleaming cars, and two-story houses painted a picture that put some fear into the players as they gawked out the car windows.

"Man," Bobby exclaimed. "Did you see that Mustang? That's my dream car. A red one, just like that."

"It's your dream car all right. You'll never have a car like that," Johnny said.

"What do people do in those gigantic houses?" Penny asked absently.

"Big parties," Don replied.

"Big kitchens?" Scott wondered.

"Lots of cars in the garages," Bobby commented.

Then Mike added, "I don't know. It takes a lot of work to keep up that lifestyle. People like that have to get rich or try dying."

Johnny caught it. "What? Try dying? I think that is what we are doing today, not the rich folks."

Everyone cracked up and slapped Mike on the back.

Finally, on the court for warm-ups, the daydreaming turned to anger as the Woodlake team made the astute observation that Johnson had a girl on their team.

"Look you guys," came the first jab. "It's the Johnson Chicas!"

"Yeah," came another, "an entire team of chicas."

"Shut the—" came a quick reply from Ramon.

Marty's head whipped around when he heard his team yelling cuss words across the court. The Woodlake players were laughing, but Ramon walked right on their half of the court and confronted the leader. Before he could spit out anything more, Marty was at his side, leading him back to the bench.

Marty gathered the team and tried to calm them down, but as the game got started, it became insult ping-pong rather than basketball. Neither team was playing the game while both sides built up baseless bravado.

At the first quarter break, Marty got down on one knee and addressed the team. "Listen, guys. You are letting them get to you. They are getting in your heads, and you cannot stoop to their level. Play your game."

He stopped and looked each player in the eye. "You are a match for them on the court. Put your anger into your play. Sure, you hate their insults, but use that energy to play your best and outplay them. That's the only defense you need. Winning this game will shut them down just fine. Got it?"

"But, Coach, did you hear what they said about Penny? We can't let that go, Coach." it was Scott's red face that revealed that Penny was growing on him.

"Yes, I heard them," Marty said. "Our best answer? Put her in at just the right time and prove them wrong. We all know she is a better shooter than any of them. Soon enough they will get that. Soon enough."

Back on the court, the team put the insults out of their heads. Still tempted to throw an occasional elbow, they could hear Marty's voice in their heads and got focused.

During one time-out, Johnny breathlessly asked, "When will you put her in?"

"Wait for it" was the reply.

During the second quarter, the score bounced back and forth for the lead. When the score tied at 10–10, Marty subbed in Penny for Scott and the rhythm of the game changed.

The Woodlake players were slow to adapt from taunting to simple basketball. The insults and trash talk flowed as their own cleverness and self-importance spurred them on. Marty's tactic was working. They were overconfident and distracted.

Looking over at the Woodlake coach, Marty saw total indifference to the abuse being thrown around by his team. Marty watched the lame excuse for a coach never address the language or insults. In fact, he seemed to be amused by it.

From the sideline, Marty emphasized basics and strategy to score points. "Johnny, steal the ball. They are dribbling all over the place. Don, get those rebounds. You are taller than anyone on their team. Bobby, go for those outside shots. You are on fire!"

Woodlake never saw it coming. Penny's perfect outside shots and layups dominated the second half and confused the heck out of the overconfident home team. The madder they got, the worse they played. The confusion, not to mention their disbelief that a girl could play, put the Jags in perfect position to go ahead, and stay ahead.

The Jags won their third game. Three more than anyone thought possible.

Stunned, the Woodlake team walked across the court to the doors of the gym, forgoing the customary high-five ritual.

"Where were the refs?" they murmured.

"Can you believe how those guys can cuss?"

"How bad must their school be if they have to play a girl?"

"Did you notice she wasn't even a starter? Pathetic," rang out the justifications as they trailed out of the gym.

Another win, another celebration at A&W.

As they drove up, Marty said, "I will go broke if you guys keep winning!"

They all laughed, and Ramon added, "Better get another part-time job, Coach."

They sat down with root beer in hand and chatted about the game and insults they had to endure from the Woodlake team.

"Doesn't it tick you off, Coach? Don't you just get mad and want to go punch somebody?" Ramon asked. "Have you ever lost it in a game? I mean like got really mad and lost your cool?"

Marty suppressed a sarcastic laugh. "Well," he started, trying to figure out how to tell the story. "There was this one time. A lot of times, but this was the worst, or maybe the best."

He took a sip of root beer and dove in. "It was a summer league in high school. I was on a pretty good team. We had about three guys over six feet. But we met our match when we played against Elk Grove."

The team nodded, acknowledging the rep of athletes from Elk Grove. They were big country boys.

"Yeah, so they had three guys close to seven feet, the least of which was Bill Cartwright. At the time, he was all-state and then went to USF."

"Oh my gosh," they all said at once.

"Yeah, we were up against it. Fortunately, Cartwright was kind of fooling around, not taking us too seriously, so we were competitive, you know, keeping up with them."

"Wow," Penny chimed in. "That must have felt good."

"It did," he answered her optimistic take on things. "Until it didn't."

They all groaned in anticipation of the rest of the story.

"The stress was building because Elk Grove was messing around and the refs weren't calling anything. We were getting beat up and madder by the minute. So, I was jumping up to grab a rebound, just slightly ahead of Cartwright. He was behind me and jumping for the ball. He is about a foot taller than me, right? So, he comes down with the ball and his giant bony elbow slams into the side of my face. It felt like a gunshot, or at least what I thought a gunshot would feel like." Marty rubbed his cheekbone in memory of Bill Cartwright's elbow.

The team winced in sympathy.

"Man, it hurt like crazy, but the ref didn't call it. Then my teammate was so mad he jumped on another player's back, feet dangling off the floor, and started punching his head. It was nuts. We were all so mad. Then the whistle blows, and the ref calls a technical and throws my teammate out of the game."

"Figures," Johnny moaned, shaking his head.

"Yeah, it was bad. I had the ball and the ref motions for me to give it to him. My face is throbbing, and I am steaming mad. I was about four feet from the ref, and I threw the ball with two hands as hard as I could at the ref, blasting the ball right into his chest."

All eyes popped, and mouths gaped.

"Totally knocked the breath out of him. He couldn't even call a technical on me because he couldn't breathe."

"Did you get to keep playing?" Don asked.

"No, the other ref threw me out," Marty said, shaking his head at the memory.

Ramon lifted his hand for a high five. "Wow, Coach, good for you! That must have felt great!"

"No, it didn't feel great. I was out of the game. My teammate was out of the game, and we lost. I was out of control and hurt our team. Didn't help in any way."

"Yeah, but you got some justice, right?" Don reasoned. "Putting that ref on his heels."

Marty said, "Nope, no justice at all. If I would have focused on the game, we could have won, or at least made a showing. That would have been justice. As it was, that team scored on the technical free throws and our two top scorers were out in the parking lot."

It had to be hard to fathom. Their coach, so calm and tough, had a temper that got the better of him.

He scratched the back of his head, trying to make the story a warning. "We could have made a good showing against the best team in the league. Instead, we ended up embarrassed and never recovered. The summer was a bust."

"Yeah, but Coach. You showed that ref!" Johnny said with satisfaction.

"No, I didn't. He showed me. I was out of control, and he showed me the parking lot."

At the next practice, Marty arrived to see Scott watching Bobby and Johnny messing around on the playground hoop.

"It would be fun to have a cousin my own age." Scott brushed his blond hair out of his eyes.

Marty looked down at him with sympathy. "No cousins?"

Scott shook his head. "No. Just sisters. Older sisters."

Marty sensed a sadness about Scott; like someone who was always on the outside looking in. He would bet that Scott was not aware of how the other kids admired him. His good looks, athleticism, and cool manner, all things every twelve-year-old longed for. *Maybe we are all on the outside looking in,* he thought. *We all think we are freaks, especially at this age.*

They entered the multipurpose room and were joined by the rest of the team. Marty assembled a string of cones across the baseline under the basket.

"He's always inventing some kind of torture for us," Bobby said with a sigh.

Marty called the group together and lined them up on the baseline opposite the cones. "Okay, guys, let's get warmed up."

After dividing the team into two groups, he herded them to the other end of the court, then lined them up on both corners of the key.

"Okay, every time you score, you run to the other end of the court, grab a cone, then run back and put the cone behind your team. Every once in a while, I will change the place where you shoot from. One ball per team. Everyone shoots."

It took a few minutes to control the complaining and trash talk, but Marty knew instinctively that competition was a good way to get their juices flowing.

"Good job on the drill, guys," he encouraged. "Before we work on our layups and outside shots, I want to try a new play."

The team hustled over to Marty, unable to hide their eagerness to learn something new. Marty smiled with satisfaction as he watched them, excited about learning. *Couldn't ask for more*, he thought with a surprising amount of pride.

Marty stood outside the baseline with the ball and instructed Scott. "You just scored, and I am the opposing team trying to throw an inbound pass back to my player." Marty tossed the ball to Scott, posing as the opponent, and encouraged him to make his way back to his own end of the court.

Scott trotted off down the court and made an easy shot in his own basket.

Marty called him back. "Let's try it another way."

Scott came back down the court and handed the ball to Marty. "Everyone pick someone to guard. Ramon, you guard Scott. Don't let him catch the inbound pass I'm trying to get to him." Marty added one more thing. "Oh yeah. I only have five seconds to get the ball in-bounds. If I can't get it to my player in five seconds, it goes to the other team."

He lifted the ball to his chest and attempted the inbound pass to Scott. Ramon stood behind Scott and tried to swipe the ball away. Scott was too quick. He caught the pass, pivoted, and headed back down the court.

"Okay, try again."

Scott threw the ball back to Marty.

"This time, Ramon, get between me and Scott. Use your arms to disrupt the pass."

Ramon looked confused but tried it. He flailed his arms around Scott but was watching Marty. Scott moved over a few steps and could catch the pass from Marty.

"Try again," Marty said. "Don't watch me, Ramon. Watch Scott."

This time, Ramon kept his back to Marty and put pressure on Scott to disrupt the pass. "That's it, Ramon. Keep the pressure on him."

Marty explained peripheral vision. "Have one eye on where the ball is and the other on where the ball is going."

The team stared at him, not sure what he was talking about.

It was Penny who piped up. "Like my mom, right? She is always keeping an eye on what I'm doing and where I'm going at the same time!"

They nodded and continued to practice being aware of what was going on around them. They kept up the new defense, practicing it with all the players. With their conditioning improving, this defensive press would come in handy.

Chapter 15

Chasing the Hot Dog

Marty sat at the kitchen table and fiddled with the slight tear in the plastic tablecloth. With the phone balanced between his ear and his shoulder, he bounced his foot nervously on the floor. He nodded absently as the voice on the end of the line explained that he was a reporter for the *Sacramento Bee* newspaper.

"So, Marty. I heard about the girl on your team. Unusual, I'd say. How did it happen that you let her play?" he asked.

"I'd be crazy to not let her play, Mr. Bennet. She is our best player," Marty answered.

"I see," he said, apparently unconvinced. "But no one in the Sacramento school district has a girl on any team. How did she land on yours? Have there been any objections? Have there been complaints?"

"Not really. When people get to know Penny, see her play, they aren't too concerned about eligibility. She is fun to watch and adds a great element to our team."

There was a slight pause that Marty interpreted as the reporter from the *Bee* trying to think of something else to ask.

Bennet cleared his throat. "Let me ask you this. Who approached you about allowing a girl on the team? ERA supporters? Women's lib folks? Were you approached by anti-ERA factions? Title 9 advocates? Anyone voicing interest in the political nature of this?"

Marty grabbed the receiver from his shoulder and stood up. "Look, I think you have the wrong idea. Penny approached me. She wanted to play. There are no girls' teams. Heck, there wasn't even a boys' team at Johnson until this year." He paced around the kitchen as far as the coiled phone cord would let him.

"If you want to know anything about Penny, I'll tell you. She is a sweet kid, works hard, plays well, and loves sports. She is from a family with a lot of heartache. Penny lives in that environment, and I think it helps her cope. She experiences a lot of joy when she plays. It is infectious for all of us. Every kid on our team is from overwhelming life circumstances, and sports are a healthy way for them to manage the craziness at home." He stopped short, realizing he was preaching.

"I'm sorry, Marty," the reporter said kindly. "It is so unusual that I thought there might be more to the story."

Marty took a breath. "There is more to the story. These kids, from unique backgrounds and different life circumstances, are enjoying playing ball, improving their skills, and being a team."

The call carried on for a while, and Marty felt good about it when he hung up the phone. *He probably won't even print it because it isn't juicy enough, or controversial enough, to interest anyone.*

Every day after that, he scoured the sports pages of the *Bee*, just out of curiosity. For weeks, he didn't see a word about Penny, Johnson Elementary, or anything about sixth-grade sports.

But a few weeks later, he happened on a small article in the neighborhood advertising circular, with a headline that read: "Local Girl Makes the Team." The article—if you could call it that—didn't mention Penny by name, or Marty, or Johnson. Just a brief human-interest anecdote that no one would really care about or notice.

What a day. One for the books, Marty thought as he threw textbooks on his bed to emphasize its end. He got ready for practice, hoping some exercise would turn his day around. That chem lab was ridiculous, not to mention that poli-sci was about as boring as watching the six o'clock news.

"Three more years of this," he muttered as he tied his shoes and stood to leave for practice. "Grandma," he said as he moved to the front door, "I'm going to the school for practice. I'll be back for dinner." He looked back at his grandmother, engrossed in *The Merv Griffin Show*. "It smells terrific, by the way."

She looked up and smiled. "We will feast when you return. Have fun."

"Hmm, fun. That would be a novel idea," he mused. When he opened the door, the sound sent Grandma's black-and-white Brittany spaniel, Perky, scampering from the food dish in the kitchen to Marty's feet with the exuberant hope of an outing.

Marty bent down and gave the dog a scratch behind the ear. "Now you would make basketball practice interesting."

"You should let those kids chase Perky around for a while," Grandma suggested. "That would get them in shape in a hurry."

"Not a bad idea," Marty said.

Finding the dog's leash took a minute, as he hadn't been on a walk in ages. Finally, Marty clipped it on Perky's collar, made a stop in the kitchen, then headed out the door toward the school.

Perky was cute, but out of control. Whenever he had the chance, the dog ran crazed. He ran at the speed of light when let off the leash. Heaven help anyone who accidentally left the front door open. Marty, frustrated with everything about the dog, including the name his grandma insisted on, had all but given up on training the nutcase.

He often thought "Frenzy" would be a better name, like the

Hitchcock horror film. That was what Perky had become, a horror.

The team, gathered outside the gym, laughed hysterically when they saw their coach being dragged down the street by the wild spaniel.

"All right," Marty said as he approached the group. "You won't be laughing for long, believe me."

He motioned for the team to follow him to the baseball field. It was a brisk January day, but the sun was out, and they had about an hour to make the most of the workout.

Marty stood with the little dog at the edge of the pavement where the field started and pointed her toward the chain-link fence about fifty yards out. "Okay, when I say go, I want Penny, Johnny, and Scott to run and catch Perky. The rest of you stay here. Your job is to keep Perky from getting on the pavement, so you chase him back toward the fence."

The team stared at him.

"This makes no sense, Coach," Scott complained. "We'll do all the work, catching the dog while the rest just stand here."

"We will switch it up. You will all get a turn." He added, "In fact, let's put something on the line. Anyone who successfully catches him will get a milkshake at A&W after our next win."

"I thought you were going broke, Coach?" Scott said with some attitude.

Marty got ready to let Perky go. "Don't worry, you won't catch him."

After a few more instructions, he let Perky off the leash and sent the first wave after him. It was a mad race chasing a black-and-white flash across the field. Those kids never got close until Perky reached the fence, turned, and ran along its width, then let them chase him some more.

Like a rocket, he headed back to the group on the pavement. The first group bent over, holding their sides, desperate for a breath, while the rest of the team did their best to not let Perky pass them.

Darting and weaving across the field, they chased the little dog, who ran like wildfire.

Perky made a sweet pivot and headed back across the field toward the fence.

Marty hollered to the first group, "Chase him back!"

The fence group waited for him to get close and then chased him back to the second group, all hoping to be the one to catch him, to be the fastest. But all they could do was wrangle him toward the second group. They rested for a few seconds while the others worked at keeping him from getting on the pavement.

"Keep him on the grass," Marty instructed, knowing that if the dog got past those kids, they would probably never see him again.

The "drill" lasted an hour. Perky never stopped; never even slowed down.

Ramon stood, bent over with his hands on his thighs, gasping for breath. "I'll bet you can't even catch him, Coach."

"What will you bet?" Marty asked with a grin.

Ramon knew better than to bet against Coach. The team watched Perky make another sprint across the field. Then, astonished, they watched him turn around and run back when he heard Marty whistle. He pulled out a hot dog from his pocket and easily clipped the leash on Perky's collar. He let him enjoy the hot dog on the grass at the feet of the dog-tired team.

"You had that all along!" Scott complained, red-faced and winded.

"Yeah," Marty answered. "It's the only trick I have."

The team, with exhaustion compounded by aching legs and strained lungs, added to their frustration as they watched Perky lie contentedly, eating his treat.

"That hot dog is kind of like a dog's version of a root beer float," Mike chuckled.

"Hey, guys." Don grinned. "Why don't blind guys parachute jump?"

The team looked at him.

"Why don't blind guys like to parachute jump?" With no takers, he added, "Because it scares the bananas out of their dogs."

Johnny suppressed a grin, apparently not wanting to give Don the satisfaction of making him laugh. Penny's giggle, prompted by her kindness, made it even funnier.

Scott couldn't let it go. "Don, you give new meaning to the word 'dork.'"

Don smiled. "Yeah, I know. That joke was a real dog."

Chapter 16

Arkansas, 1994
Seventeen Years after the Murder

The January air blew cold and clean on his face as Dean barreled down the highway at seventy miles an hour.

The Kawasaki K2 650 was not the perfect bike, but it was beautiful all the same. He had decided the helmet, fastened to the rear seat, would stay there for the time being, maybe forever. He had a hardy pair of goggles to shield his eyes from bugs and dirt.

He'd headed from his dingy apartment in town to a quiet road nearby to try out his new girl. That was what he was calling it; his "new girl."

He had bought the bike the day before with skimmed and stolen dollars from over the last few years. The last hundred dollars came from his girlfriend's secret stash of tip money hidden in a jar in the back of the closet. "Hidden" was a bit of an exaggeration. He had always known about it and had raided the jar when this sweet deal presented itself. It wouldn't take her long to figure it out, so he was pretty sure he would need a "new girl."

The main street through town gave way to an empty country road. It called to him, promising freedom and power. He gunned the engine and sped up, feeling the adrenaline stoke his nerves. He continued to speed up, unable to contain the rush, but oblivious to the rain that had turned into an icy sleet.

He didn't notice the old pickup that appeared on the horizon until it was too late. The bike struggled to grip the road. It was the bike that slid first, throwing its rider then sliding across the narrow road as if propelled by some unseen force.

The truck driver reacted, slamming on his worn brakes only to hit the rider and drag him under the tires as the truck careened into the ditch. What had been blind exhilaration was now motionless and black.

His eyes opened to the unfamiliar sound of machines beeping and pumping, the nauseating smell of disinfectant, and searing pain in his legs that brought him to full consciousness.

He tried to sit up. "Where am I? What is going on?" He cried out as he struggled to get the leverage needed to sit upright. His cries went unheard as he sat alone on the bed in the sterile hospital room. It didn't take long to discover the horrible truth.

Both legs gone below the knee.

Chapter 17

David and Goliath

David Ramon slid unnoticed onto the back pew of the church. Mass was almost over as he scanned the familiar bowed heads stretched across the narrow church. All eyes were closed as the priest chanted the closing blessing, giving David the chance to spot his mother.

As much as he hated Mass, he really loved this building. The Spanish-style white adobe exterior stood stately and proud in the run-down neighborhood. Inside, the sanctuary transformed the chaotic everyday life to a place of calm and safety. Its wooden arches spaced across the towering ceiling were painted the color of a soothing clear blue sky. Behind the priest, the curved apse housed the life-size ceramic statue portraying the sad and dejected Christ. David's dad often joked that it depicted well the suffering congregation.

It was the stained-glass windows on either side of the pews that always captured David's wandering imagination. Intricate colored glass illustrated stories from the Bible. It felt hypnotizing, staring into those windows, watching the light from outside blast through and bring the stories to life.

As the blessing ended, he lowered his head and kept it bowed as his mother, aunts, and cousins stood, flipped up the kneeler, and scooted to the center aisle. Only when the parishioners crossed themselves and turned to leave did David lift his head and make eye contact with his mother. Her disdainful look proved that his little act wasn't fooling her.

He joined her in the aisle, then walked to the double oak doors, down the steps, and out onto the sidewalk.

David felt pressure to attend church from his mother and pressure to skip church like his dad and uncles always did. The proverbial rock and a hard place. As the group made their way home, David spotted the men. There they were, waiting in the backyard, with the grill fired up. The aroma filled the neighborhood with the familiar mouthwatering smell of Sunday lunch.

They were grilling elote, David's favorite—corn on the cob, smothered in butter, mayo, Cotija cheese, chili powder, and lime. All the cousins clamored to the grill to grab their elote and gnaw on it while they waited for the rest of the food to appear on tables covered in colorful tablecloths.

The moms brought out the lunch and set up the spread. The hungry crowd gathered at the tables to feast on tamales, chili rellenos, and rice and beans, along with warm flour tortillas. At the end of the line lay the best of the lot; homemade churros.

David's stomach growled while he made every attempt to appear cool around his uncles. He was one of the oldest of the cousins, and he had a reputation to uphold. All the same, he couldn't help elbowing his way into the front of the line.

"So, what were you up to, David?" his mother asked.

Try as he might to avoid her, she had plopped down right beside him in one of the frayed, webbed lawn chairs.

"Sorry, Mom," he said. "I'm on the basketball team at school now, and I wanted to play a little this morning for practice."

"Play a little? Those boys who play pickup games on Sunday mornings are not the kids to hang around with. They are a pack of wolves, David. Wolves! They are in high school and up to no good." She paused and caught her breath. "Not going to church with your family is one thing that I am not happy about but hanging around that bunch is dangerous." She lowered her voice and said, "I'm glad you are playing basketball, but please stay away from those older boys."

She stood and moved away toward the other moms, leaving David feeling annoyed and a little guilty.

"David!" His uncle motioned for him to come over to the grill where empty beer bottles were accumulating on the lawn.

"Yeah?" He secretly relished the feeling of being included with the men.

Uncle Carlos, however, was a particularly hard nut, who usually liked nothing more than to make David feel stupid.

"Come here, kid. I want to ask you something." Carlos gestured again for David to come over.

David could tell they were all a little drunk and the closer he got, the more he realized he was not being invited over to join them, but to be the butt of some joke. Of all the cousins, he was the one Carlos liked to mess with. Thanks to him, these Sunday gatherings usually deteriorated into a painful experience.

Sheepishly, David wandered over. "What?" he asked, recognizing his uncle's grin. *Here it comes*, he thought.

"I hear you're playing basketball. I can't for the life of me get why anyone would want you on a team? You might be tall but come on, you are such a spaz, man." He laughed out loud and looked to his companions for approval. "Am I right? David playing basketball? Remember that time he tripped over a crack in the sidewalk and flew headfirst into the chain-link fence?" He threw his head back and laughed at the story that he never tired of telling.

"Lay off, Carlos." It was David's dad who intervened. "David, go help your mom clean up," he said dismissively.

David slinked away, feeling the sting of his uncle's insults, not to mention the orders to help the women.

Marty left church that Sunday, thinking about the team. The pastor had told the story of David and Goliath, which stimulated his thoughts. Marty had never attended Sunday school, so it was new to him. *So true to life,* he thought. *We really are up against it. Our game this week with Noralto might not qualify as Goliath, but they are probably better than Johnson. Although, a Goliath or two are coming soon enough.*

The drive home was consumed with thoughts about how to win the next game. Marty's instincts immediately went to strategy. He'd taught the team the press, but they hadn't executed it in a game. He got out of the car, then headed up to the house thinking about the pastor's words: "David was clever enough but motivated more by his faith in God than his own abilities."

Marty went inside and was standing by the living room window looking out on the street, deep in thought, when he saw David Ramon walking down the sidewalk toward his car. He started to go back outside and then stopped when David approached his car then looked in the open passenger-side window.

Marty assumed David didn't know where he lived but recognized the Dodge Demon. Everyone recognized the Demon. David stood there looking in the car through the window, and Marty remembered he had left his tape player on the seat.

Oh, man. I better get out there. As he stepped outside, Marty saw Ramon look up and down the street, then back to the open window.

Before he could reach in, Marty walked up behind him and said, "Hey Ramon, what's up?"

Startled, Ramon took a second to gain his wits. Marty expected a lame excuse of some kind but was surprised to hear him say, "Well, to be honest, I was going to take your tape player. I changed my mind, though. I think it's a piece of junk, anyway." His bravado faded, and he looked down at his feet, unable to maintain eye contact.

"Hmm," Marty said. "Well, I'm glad you changed your mind. I don't have many tapes, but that crummy tape player is all I have to play them on."

Ramon grinned in appreciation. "Sorry, Coach. I guess you aren't having any better luck with your car than you are with your team."

"Your team, Ramon. It's your team. And I think you guys are shaping up to be pretty good."

"Sure, Coach. Whatever you say. I gotta go."

Marty smiled and let him go on his way. "See you tomorrow at practice."

Ramon looked back at the white guy who'd just let him off the hook. "Later, man," he said with a nod.

Marty watched him walk away. Another disaster averted.

A few days later, Principal Gould called Marty to talk to him about David Ramon.

"His grades are horrible, Marty. I can't see letting him play basketball when he is failing sixth grade."

Marty slumped at the news. He held the phone and stared out the window, searching for the right words. "I understand, Mrs. Gould. Basketball is not the biggest priority for a twelve-year-old." He paused while he gathered his thoughts. "Our team is pretty bad but getting better. David is important to us, but I think the team is important to him, too." He scratched the back of his head. "Being on the team is good for David . . . for all the kids. Winning isn't the most important thing, but maybe learning something new, working together, having fun, is important." Marty took a breath. "I know what it's like, Mrs. Gould, to have something you love taken away. Maybe it helps these kids to do better in school, not worse."

He wasn't sure if the silence on the other end of the line meant she was mad, or just thinking. Bucking up his courage, he added, "I'm not trying to tell you how to do your job. You know these kids better than I do. I'm just saying maybe the team could be an incentive to work on his grades."

"Thanks, Marty." Her tone had lightened a little, allowing him to relax. "I appreciate your care for David and the team. Let's stay the course. I will work with him on the grades. You keep him motivated on the court. How does that sound?"

"Sounds great." He hung up the phone with a sigh of relief.

I guess I'm on the hook for this kid. No pressure. No pressure at all.

The next game, against Noralto, was well underway, with the score bouncing back and forth from the get-go. Neither team seemed to have an advantage. Marty felt some encouragement that the team was taking shots, although they were mostly bricks. The refs didn't help matters, missing obvious fouls and nitpicking at things that should have been overlooked with twelve-year-olds learning the game.

"Coach, did you see that?" Johnny yelled as he came to the sidelines for the half. A string of cusswords flew from his mouth as his frustration hit its peak.

"Okay, Johnny, enough with the language," Marty said.

The usually tolerant Don stepped in. "Yeah, Coach. That number twenty has elbowed me so many times. I swear I'm gonna let him have it."

"Okay, okay," Marty said calmly. "I get it, they are obnoxious, and the refs are blind. But this is what we have to work with. If we let them get under our skin, we will lose this game. Remember Woodlake?"

The sweat-soaked team flopped on the folding chairs set up on their sideline. They shook their heads, feeling hamstrung by the injustices of the refs. Marty stood tall over them, searching for a way to inspire.

He knelt on one knee. "Pull in close, guys." He motioned as they reluctantly pulled their chairs in close.

Marty attempted to calm them down and give some perspective. "They have got Penny double-teamed," he explained. "Somehow, they figured out how to stop her. We have to score some other way."

Marty looked up at the scoreboard, then back at the team. "We have to outthink these guys if we are going to win. It's critical that we don't lose our heads. Our offense isn't working, so we are going to have to focus on our defense."

The buzzer sounded, calling the players back into the game. Marty watched for a few minutes and realized he had emphasized defense but still needed to help them put their press into play. He called a time-out and gathered the team around him.

"Scott, you take the ball out on the sideline and get it to Johnny. Johnny, I want you to dribble up the court then pass the ball out of bounds under the basket. Noralto will get the ball, you set up the press. Pressure them, get a steal, then a layup."

"But, Coach," Scott protested. "That will never work. It's crazy! That's throwing the ball away. They will go ahead."

Marty looked at the rest of the players. "Trust me on this. Set up the press close to the basket, and you'll have a better chance of scoring using good defense to get control of the ball." He looked directly at Scott. "And we will go ahead."

They nodded reluctantly.

Then Ramon spoke up. "Are you sure we can't just, as Don would say, beat the bananas out of them and teach them a lesson?"

Marty smiled. "Sure, and then we get kicked out of the league. I want you to play smart. We don't want to get even. We want to win!"

The ref gave Scott the ball on the sideline. He passed it to

Johnny, who dribbled down court to their own basket. He stopped to make a pass, purposely overthrowing Ramon, and the ball went out of bounds under the basket. A cheer went up from the Noralto fans, and Johnny fumed. Noralto passed the ball to their best player, who ran down court and broke the press. The two-point advantage frustrated the Jags, and Johnny looked at the coach with that "what the heck?" look on his face.

Near the end of the fourth quarter, they tied the score at 14–14. A Noralto player stepped out of bounds while dribbling the ball down court. The ref called it and handed the ball to Scott on the sideline.

Marty, standing nearby, said to Johnny, "Don't waste time arguing. Throw it out of bounds under their basket and use the press."

Scott, shaking his head, reluctantly threw the ball to Johnny, who obediently passed it over Ramon's head and out of bounds. This time the Jags, in a moment of uncommon clarity, set up the defensive press and tied up the ball. Bobby got a steal, dribbled down to his own basket, and bounce-passed it to Penny, whose usual defenders had panicked and taken their eyes off her. Big mistake.

Marty saw the coach of the opposing team out of the corner of his eye. His frustrated body language told Marty the press had worked. Penny dribbled a few steps and took a bank shot off the backboard, landing the game-winning basket.

As the buzzer sounded to end the game, the Jags went ballistic. They had, against all probability, racked up another win, putting them four and one in the league.

The celebration kicked into high gear, but Marty slumped down in the chair on the sideline. For a moment, he felt tired. Every muscle went slack and useless. All the air in the room evaporated, and he felt alone on the surface of the moon. He knew he should jump for joy like the rest of the team, but he couldn't move.

The conflict that arose within confused him. *We won—again!*

But, at this moment, he physically felt the effects of the effort it took. The stress of keeping these kids focused, thirty-two solid minutes of pure adrenaline coursing through his body. Every game, hard fought; every point, crucial; every strategy, a gamble.

He lifted his head in time to see the team continuing their frenetic revelry. *Pure joy*, he thought. *They are having fun, growing, caring about each other, learning.*

Maybe winning is too important to me. The sermon on Sunday came back to mind and reminded him to be aware of his motivation. Eventually, he was able to get up and join the team, with high fives and the nagging suspicion that he didn't have enough money on him to make another trip to A&W.

After Marty rooted through his car to find some change under the floor mat, the celebration and debrief continued over root beer.

Johnny, still feeling he looked bad in the game, worked to keep his chin up. "Did they even get what we did, Coach?" Johnny seemed to be afraid that no one had noticed his sacrifice.

"Doesn't matter, Johnny," Marty said with a sigh of relief. "It worked, and it was amazing."

"That was so cool." Penny could barely contain herself. "They didn't see that coming at all."

"Yeah, maybe," Johnny added. "But I still looked like an idiot."

Marty smiled. "Not to the scoreboard, Johnny. And not to any of us."

A small garden spot along the side of the house needed weeding, and Grandma wanted Marty to get it ready to plant some flowers. The dirt was dry and hard, and he stabbed it with the sharp end of his shovel. Sweat trickled down his neck as he continued to dig up dead plants, rocks, and weeds. He slammed the shovel in and hoisted the dirt into a wheelbarrow.

The plan: sift out the weeds and rocks, mix in some good topsoil, then throw it back on the bed, getting it ready to plant later.

Grandma stood on the porch, leaning over the rail and watching him work. He knew she was appreciative, but the scowl gave away her irritation at the way he was going about the job. He ignored the pained expression and was glad to hear the phone ring, luring her back inside.

"Hi, Coach!" he heard from a distance.

He looked up to see Penny waving from the sidewalk. She was climbing off her beat-up Schwinn, undoubtedly handed down from older siblings.

He put the shovel into the dirt and rested on the wood handle. "Hey, Penny. What are you up to?"

"I just shot one hundred layups in my backyard!" she declared proudly. "There was no one home today, so I had the hoop all to myself."

Marty looked at her with astonishment. "One hundred?"

"Yep. No one guarding me, so I made most of them."

Marty laughed. "You're amazing, Penny. I imagine the rest of the team home watching *Starsky and Hutch*, all sprawled out on the floor eating ice cream and popcorn."

Penny smiled. "You're working hard, Coach. What are you doing?"

Marty looked down at the half-weeded plot of ground and groaned. "Helping my grandma." He motioned for her to come over. "You can help, if you want."

Penny eagerly walked across the little yard to help.

Marty looked at the wheelbarrow. "If you could dig out the rocks and weeds, that would help a lot."

"Sure, Coach," she agreed and dug into the work with enthusiasm.

Marty could tell she did a lot of work at home, as she tackled the job with no questions or hesitation.

The pair worked steadily, getting the flower bed ready for planting. Penny chatted nonstop as Marty listened to one story after another about the difficulties of life in a big family.

"They all think it's funny that I'm playing on the team," Penny said, a little sheepishly.

"Have they ever seen you play?" Marty dumped a bag of new dirt into the flower bed.

"Nah," she answered.

"Well, if they saw you play, they wouldn't be laughing." Marty looked at his star player. "You're our ringer, you know."

Penny didn't look up. "They would just say it's a loser team, not to mention I'm just a girl."

Marty thought for a minute. "We have only lost once, and you didn't even play in that game. I'd say we are a pretty good team, and you are a talented basketball player. Like I said, if they saw you, they would be proud."

"It looks like this bed is almost ready. Are you going to finish it now or later?" She glanced up at the darkening sky.

"Well, I should finish it tonight because I have church tomorrow." Marty reached for another bag of dirt.

"Church? You go to church?" Penny asked with some doubt. "Does your grandmother make you?"

Marty laughed. "No, she doesn't go. I go because I like it."

Penny looked at him doubtfully. "My mom wants us to go to church, but most of the time we don't. There's always a fight about it."

"Yeah, that would really be hard. You've got to want to go, or it can be painful. Kind of like school." Marty continued to work, emptying a few bags of dirt into the flower bed. His mind was racing. It was never easy to talk to kids about his faith. "It started being fun for me a few years ago when I almost got eaten by a bear," he said casually as he watched her gasp.

"What!" she exclaimed. "Really, a bear?"

"Yeah, the day after I hit a guy with my truck. He had just robbed a 7-Eleven."

Penny looked up, wide eyed. "I guess that would make you want to go to church!"

Marty told Penny the story of the robbery and the camping trip, and how he started reading the Bible.

"Until then, I never went to church or even thought about spiritual things. I never really saw the point. Once I started reading the Bible and talking to my friends about God, I wanted to know more."

"What is there to know?" Penny asked. "I thought when you died you kind of got swallowed up and disappeared into the night." The faraway look in her eyes revealed an uncommon pain. She looked at Marty and said, "I'm not being a smart aleck. I don't understand it."

Marty sat down on the grass and asked, "Do you want to know more about God, Penny?"

Penny sat down too. "Well yeah. I believe in God and all. I just figured I'm not good enough. You know, I don't go to Sunday school or anything."

Marty took a deep breath and dove in. "Let me explain it like this. Most of us think that if we could be really good, like extra nice or give all our money away, stuff like that, God would like us."

Penny nodded.

"But here's the thing, Penny. God loves us when we are at our absolute worst. He created us, He is always with us, and He loves us no matter how far away from Him we are."

Penny's eyes conveyed some skepticism.

"Jesus died on the cross so we could have a relationship with God the Father. On our own, we really aren't good enough. We are too imperfect to have a relationship with a holy, perfect God. Jesus's death and resurrection made it so we could know God."

Penny looked down and pulled some grass out of the ground and played with it. "I've heard that before, but I don't get why Jesus had to die? That doesn't make sense to me. Why didn't God save

Him from that?"

Marty smiled at Penny's obvious intelligence, along with her nature to be polite. She had experienced a lot in life that would not make sense to anyone, let alone a twelve-year-old.

She started again. "I mean the whole cross thing. I have always thought it was a terrible story."

"Well, you are right, Penny. It is terrible. Yet, at the same time, it is the best story ever," Marty said. "I can put it simply, but it really isn't simple. Jesus was perfect. He had no sin. He was a perfect sacrifice for our sin so we could have a relationship with a perfect God."

She looked confused, so Marty said, "You play softball, right?" Penny perked up. "Yeah, I love softball."

"Has your coach ever asked you to lay down a sacrifice bunt?"

"Sure. I can bunt pretty good."

Marty went on, "Do you usually get out when you do that?"

"Yeah, usually, but it is on purpose so the base runner can score or move to the next base."

"How does it make you feel when you do that? When you get out on purpose?" Marty asked.

"It's okay. I don't mind because it is for the team. It's to win the game." She smiled at the thought.

"Well," Marty said, "in a small way, that is like Jesus dying on the cross. He did it, so we would win the game. That is, have our sins forgiven." He waited for that to sink in a little. "The good news is that Jesus rose from the dead. You know—Easter. He didn't stay dead. He is alive and wants to be with us throughout life."

Penny fiddled with the grass. "Is that all there is to it? You just found this out and now you like God?"

Marty smiled. "Well, I made a choice. I decided that I wanted to give my life to Jesus. To trust Him that one day I would go to heaven to be with Him, and that in the meantime, I would live for Him here."

Penny looked at Marty with tear-filled eyes. "I want to decide that same thing, Coach," she said quietly. "I want to be in heaven someday."

Marty leaned forward a little. "Penny, you went in your back yard today and worked hard to get better at basketball. Well, becoming a Christian is nothing like that. God doesn't want your hard work and effort. He just wants you to trust Him that He loves you."

Penny blinked back her tears. "I think I understand. It is Jesus that is good enough, right? Not me. I never could be good enough even if I tried my hardest?"

Marty leaned on his elbows and smiled. "You are amazing, Penny. Most adults don't understand and yet you seem to get it." Marty went on. "A few years ago, when I started thinking about these things, I said a simple prayer. Prayer is just conversation. I said a prayer that expressed how I felt. That was the beginning of a cool change that happened to me. I'm not perfect by any means, but I think I'm a lot closer to God. I really enjoy Him and the road He has me on."

Penny was quiet for a minute. "Could you tell me how to do that, Coach? Like how you showed me how to set a screen in basketball? I always wanted to do that, but until you showed me, I was useless."

Marty smiled again. "Sure."

He led Penny in a simple prayer of faith there on the front lawn, alongside the wheelbarrow and the tilled-up flower bed, ready to receive the new plantings.

Chapter 18

Sacramento, 1978
Six Months after the Murder

Pete closed the book on the case. The thick file, bound in a three-ring binder, the "Murder Book," was closed. He set it in a cardboard box with the rest of the evidence, put the lid on, and attached a sticker over the edges that said "Unsolved" in bold, dispassionate letters. It might as well have said "Failure" with his name underneath. Instead, it was the victim, a fifteen-year-old kid, whose family found no justice.

He picked up the box, carried it to the elevator, went down to the basement and into the evidence storage. After signing it in, he carried it to the shelf that would become its home for the next twenty-five years. The box wasn't alone. The cold, gloomy room felt to him like Arlington Cemetery with its vast white headstones. Hundreds of boxes, so many unsolved crimes, so much injustice and misery.

He forced himself to leave the basement and head back to the office. There was plenty of work to do on other cases, but this one hurt, and he knew it would haunt him for a long time.

My only hope, he thought, *is that maybe new evidence will come to light. Maybe.*

Chapter 19

Hustle Points

The Jags felt small when they entered Babcock Elementary School's multipurpose room. It looked like their own multipurpose room, having made the switch that day from the third-grade recorder concert to gymnasium. It smelled of sloppy joes, the same lunch served at their own school.

Even the familiar hum of children laughing, balls bouncing, and adults shouting instructions brought no comfort. Though they had won four games so far, they were terrified of the mighty Babcock Bobcats.

It didn't take long for Scott to be distracted by the girls who came to watch the game. Don searched the crowd, presumably for his family. He looked thankful that they had not chosen this game to show up. Johnny and Ramon looked relieved and annoyed that no one from their neighborhood came to the game or even knew there was a game. Bobby, just happy to be on the team, and Penny, not distracted but focused on Babcock, watching their warm-up for clues on how to beat them. Marty didn't tell the team that Babcock was his "alma mater" and that walking into this room brought a hailstorm of memories.

The Babcock Bobcats worked their way around the warm-ups

fluidly, as if they were born to play the game. Most of the players were white, looked older than twelve, and wore sharp white jerseys with actual numbers.

"People look bigger in white," Penny commented to no one in particular.

Marty looked up and smiled at her joke that no one else got.

"Okay, guys" he encouraged. "Game faces."

He waited a minute for the kids to stop gawking and give him their attention. "You can handle these guys. You are getting better all the time. Do the things we practiced."

Marty steadied himself and sent them out for warm-ups. The Jags seemed flat-footed and fumbling, missing every shot they took. *This could be a long game*, he thought to himself.

He had coached against Babcock before, so he knew a few of the players. Every game against them had been a battle, but under closer scrutiny of this year's team, he noticed they seemed slower and less motivated.

As the Jags huddled up, Marty said, "Don't get freaked out by these guys. There's a lot of showboating going on. You guys can win this."

They formed their huddle with some reluctance. They half-heartedly shouted, "Who's next!" and went onto the court.

The jump ball went in favor of the Jags.

"Wow," Marty said out loud. "First time."

Don worked at setting screens, and Johnny successfully drove around the screen to make a layup. Defense was getting better, but still allowed a lot of scoring. Scott, like a recharged battery, engaged at a new level of energy. Marty was sure it would last as long as those girls stayed where they were.

A few harsh comments from the crowd deflected off Marty. It hadn't taken them long to realize he had switched from coaching last year's league champs to Johnson.

"Having pity on the poor kids?" or "Coaching little girls now?"

Marty ignored the insults and trash talk, but knew his team needed to step it up.

At the quarter, Marty called in the team to set up the hustle point strategy. "Okay, guys. If we are going to win this one, we've got to outhustle them. They seem kind of slow, and I think they are assuming you can't play. So let's show them."

He pulled out his clipboard and thick black marker. "Remember, one point for rebounds and one point for a blocked shot. Don and Ramon stay alert. Always be under the basket. Let's say one point for a steal. Scott, Johnny, and Penny, you've got speed over these guys. Work to steal from their point guard when he comes down court and passes to his shooters." Marty kept going. "One point for turnovers, mix it up, cause them to fumble and lose the ball. Put the pressure on. Let's say two hustle points for offensive rebounds. If we are going to miss shots, then don't give the ball away. Hustle to make a shot every time we have the ball at our end of the court."

"So, Coach," Ramon interrupted. "What do we get if we have a lot of hustle points?"

Marty looked at him for a second. "Well, you might win the game!"

The team laughed and shoved Ramon playfully.

"Okay, let's shoot for twenty-four hustle points in this game. That's what we will celebrate today. Let's say root beer floats if we hit twenty-four. Got it?"

The second quarter started up with a renewed vigor. Don and Ramon focused on rebounding when Babcock missed their shots. They were even more successful on the offensive rebounds because of their own missed shots.

"Yes!" Marty yelled when Don rebounded a long shot from Scott that bounced off the rim. Don missed his first shot but made the second one from his own rebound.

By halftime the score reflected the hustle. Marty sat the team down and commended them. He glanced over at the Babcock team and noted their heavy breathing and water guzzling.

"Okay, guys, you are doing great. Step up the pressure and let's get some steals. Penny, we will bring you in later. Our secret weapon—our closer."

Penny smiled and lowered her head in humility. This time, Penny was on the receiving end of the teasing shoves.

Into the third quarter, the score remained close.

"Bobby!" Marty hollered as he dribbled by. "Remember—head up, watch for your open man."

Bobby nodded and recognized the encouragement to shift to the right side. Bobby drew the Babcock team to the right by passing to Johnny, who returned it to Bobby. Slow and calculating, with good control of the ball on the right side of the court while Scott remained open on the left.

As Bobby saw Scott open, Don moved in for a screen. Bobby was free to pass the ball to the left and to a wide-open Scott. With miles of open court, he dribbled twice and put up a nice set shot that tied the score, 16–16.

"Yes!" Marty yelled from the sidelines, while Penny and Mike jumped up and down right beside him.

On defense, the hustle points mounted with more rebounds as Babcock unraveled a bit, watching the score inching up but still tight.

Marty overheard one Babcock player say to another, "I thought you said these guys have never played before!"

His teammate wiped the sweat from his brow and reeled off a torrent of foul language. "I heard they have a girl. What team could be good that has a girl?"

Marty turned his head a few times and scowled his best intimidation, but to no avail. It wasn't the language that bothered him; he had heard it all before. It was the insults that flew Penny's way. He could feel the veins pulsating in his neck. He took a deep breath and fought to hold back his temper. *Use it*, he said to himself.

Mike shifted on the bench beside Marty. He shouted an encouragement to the team when he wasn't wincing at the escalating trash talk.

"You know what is sad, Coach?" Mike interjected, not taking his eyes off the game.

"What's that, Mike?" Marty thought infuriating was a more appropriate sentiment.

"If those guys knew anything about Penny, they wouldn't talk about her like that."

Marty looked at his young friend. This kid, barely eleven years old, took insults and bullying every day of his life but handled it better than anyone he knew.

With the score tied at the beginning of the fourth quarter, Marty motioned to Penny. "Okay, Penny sub in for Scott."

The timing of the substitution led the Babcock team to assume Scott was getting a rest and Marty was letting the girl in for a few minutes. Their coach instructed his team to focus on guarding Don, the tall guy. Penny entered the game and held back briefly but was always open, and Bobby and Johnny passed it to her as the quarter progressed.

Still in need of hustle points, Johnny focused on getting steals. The Babcock point guard had a quick, easy dribble, but Johnny noticed he had less control over the ball on his right side.

"I'll bet he's a lefty," Johnny whispered under his breath, and zeroed in on his movements to the right. He positioned himself, reached in on the ball, then knocked it away. He caught up to the ball, dribbled down to his own basket, and scored a sweet layup with both teams left flat-footed with their mouths open at the wrong end of the court.

"That's it, Johnny! Way to keep your head up!" Marty called out and then noted the hustle point and the go-ahead basket.

Babcock was off guard now. Johnson moved the ball up and down the court like a heat-seeking missile. They passed the ball to Penny, and Penny never missed.

When the final buzzer sounded, the score stunned the crowd: 26–22. While the Babcock team and the crowd stood silent, the Johnson Jaguars went crazy. They were jumping higher, screaming louder, hugging tighter than ever before. The celebration lasted for a full five minutes, and finally Marty had to reel them in with the renewed promise of root beer floats.

As they left the school and piled into Marty's car, he couldn't help but marvel—five and one. Absolutely incredible.

Conversation at A&W turned from their amazing record to professional wrestling—universally considered a stupid sport that drew loyal fans from ages twelve to twenty and all their dads.

"Did you see the match on Saturday?" It was Bobby who brought up the subject. "Oh my gosh. 'Soul Patrol.' They are my favorite!"

"I know! Rocky Johnson, right?" It surprised Marty to hear Penny chime in. "He isn't the biggest guy out there, but he is really cut. Even my mom gets a kick out of him."

Marty had to laugh. "I like it, too. Almost as much as roller derby."

Johnny looked up and smiled. "Yeah, those chicks are awesome."

This comment caused Scott to perk up. "*Kansas City Bomber*. My favorite movie, ever."

They all started laughing at the faraway look in Scott's eyes.

Mike said, "How many movies have you seen, Scott? It couldn't be many if that's your favorite."

Penny added, "Maybe they'll make a movie about Rocky Johnson. That would be cool. He could get close to retirement, never having won a championship because the bad guys always cheat, so he trains his son who becomes a champion and makes his dad proud. Now that would be a great movie."

They all just stared at Penny.

"You are trippin', man," Johnny teased.

Don finished his homework and went out to the living room to catch his favorite TV show, which usually came on at eight. Tonight, two of his older brothers and his dad huddled around the TV watching a basketball game that had gone into overtime. Don stood in the back, waiting for his turn to watch his show.

Before long, he was riveted. His family didn't even know he knew anything about basketball. They barely acknowledged that he was on the Johnson team. Tonight, the Washington Bullets were playing the Lakers, and it was a barn burner. Don recognized immediately Elvin Hayes, the famous turnaround jumper. He was scoring at will despite the Lakers' relentless pounding away at the Bullets.

Coach Marty had told Don to go to the library and look up Elvin Hayes. Knowing Don was a bit of a bookworm, Marty encouraged him to read the story of the shy eighth grader from Louisiana who had famously gone from never having taken part in sports to becoming the first Black athlete to play at the University of Houston. Eventually, he played in the NBA.

"You will like this guy, Don," Marty had said as they were leaving the gym one day. "The Big E. I've always wondered why they call him that," he said, hoping Don would take the bait.

As Don read about this guy, the story motivated him. The inspiration was not because Don had dreams of being in the NBA but because Hayes was a tall, awkward kid who, against all odds, was a success. Elvin Hayes found what he was good at and pursued it with vigor.

His family hadn't even seemed to notice he had come into the room, and looked surprised when he shouted, "Come on, Hayes!"

All three heads turned and stared at him.

"Hayes?" Nate said, incredulously. "You airhead, he's on the Bullets."

One minor detail. His family, die-hard Laker fans, deemed all East Coast teams as the devil and his minions. Before Don could offer an explanation, they were back around screaming at the TV.

Don continued to watch, silently rooting for his hero. At the buzzer, the Lakers pulled out the win and Don's family went crazy. He waited until they left the room, then switched the channel to *Colombo*.

At Monday's practice, Don couldn't wait to impress Coach with his new info. Halfway through practice, Don plopped down next to Marty and said emphatically, "Navy aircraft carrier."

Marty turned and looked at him. "What?"

Don stood and repeated his info with pride. "The Big E. They nicknamed him after the naval aircraft carrier, *Enterprise*. You know, E equals MC2. Mass is energy. Big is better!" He beamed as he trotted across the court to join his friends.

Marty had to laugh. He had just wanted him to realize that not everyone starts out as a superstar.

Chapter 20

Sacramento, 1977
Two Months after the Murder

Pete waited as long as possible before he entered the compact interrogation room. Standard procedure . . . let 'em sweat a little. Unaffected by the ruse, Jennings waited patiently, sitting on a hard chair, arms resting on the cold metal table.

They decided that a female detective, Sergeant Sheryl Green, would conduct the intake info from Jennings and get permission for the polygraph. She was a slim blonde with kind blue eyes. No one would ever detect that she was the department's best undercover detective. Whether it was as a prostitute or tripped-out drug dealer, she was a master at makeup and changing her appearance. Today she was sweet, a little flirty, and the first face Jennings would see at the department. If she couldn't get him to take the test, no one could.

When Sheryl finished the intake, she led Jennings down the hall to an interrogation room and left him there while Pete prepared to do the primary questioning.

Pete walked in and introduced himself. "Hello, Mr. Jennings. I'm Detective Willover." He didn't reach to shake his hand but pulled out the chair opposite of Jennings and sat down. Pete took his time and stared at his notes as if he were seeing them for the first time. He wanted Jennings to think this was a routine info gathering session.

He looked at Jennings square in the face and watched for signs of stress, but he sat calmly, revealing nothing in his body language except drooping eyelids and a hint of arrogance that Pete concluded he was trying to mask.

"Have you ever been convicted of a felony, Mr. Jennings?"

Probably not expecting that to be the lead question, he hesitated for a second. "Ahh, yeah, a few years ago, falsely accused. The judge didn't believe it either. I didn't serve any time."

At least he knows enough to not deny what was easy to verify, Pete thought.

Pete continued with his questions regarding the murder and the search party. He went slowly, being careful to keep Jennings relaxed and off guard. The difficulty was that Jennings never out-and-out lied; just "adjusted" the truth. They played ping-pong back and forth, both calm, both stubborn, both very good at what they were doing.

A light tap on the door turned their attention as Sheryl stepped in. She glanced at Jennings with an almost imperceptible smile, then said, "Sal is ready, Pete."

Sal sat at a small desk next to the examination chair. He was careful to position himself so he and Jennings were not looking at each other. Before putting on the equipment, he informed Jennings of the case they were investigating. He explained in simple, straightforward terms that he had a constitutional right to have an attorney present, and he repeated the absolute voluntary nature of the test.

Jennings nodded. "Sure, whatever you say."

Stepping around the desk, Sal connected the various components to Jennings's body, hooking him up to the polygraph instrument. First was the blood-pressure cuff to monitor the continual tracing of his cardiovascular activity like heart rate and blood pressure.

Next, he fastened two rubber tubes under his shirt, around his chest and abdomen to obtain continuous breathing activity.

Last, he attached two electrodes to Jennings's fingers to get a tracing of his sweat-gland activity.

Once he was hooked up, Sal calibrated the machine to make sure everything was in working order.

Sal started the examination by asking some baseline questions that recorded Jennings's reaction when he was telling the truth. These simple questions were easy to verify, like his address and the time of day. Then Sal asked questions regarding knowledge of the victim and his whereabouts on the day of the murder.

Sal paused the questioning for a few minutes to allow Jennings to relax, then began again with questions regarding the search party and the account that Jennings had told Detective Willover.

After the second rest period, Sal continued recording Jennings's physiological responses to questions that Sal knew were true and ones that he didn't know if Jennings was lying about.

The entire thing lasted about a half hour. Jennings sat patiently while Sal removed the equipment.

"So how did I do, Doc?"

"I don't read the test. The department will get back to you." Sal motioned to the door and added, "You are free to go, sir."

Jennings walked out the door and headed down the narrow hallway and out to the street. Pete watched him strut out with a confidence that said, "You got nothing on me."

And indeed, they had nothing on him.

Chapter 21

Foul Trouble

Scott pushed the metal handle to the heavy door with all the force he could muster, as if the place were on fire. He was the first student out of the building, and he couldn't get out fast enough.

He hurried to the bike rack, pulled out his beat-up Stingray, hopped on, and sped away. *Two hours until practice*, he thought. Enough time to shake off the dust of that cramped room and the desk that wrapped around him like a straitjacket.

"School is such a drag, and sixth grade is the worst," he said out loud as he hustled down the street. He turned up Trexel Street and slowed down a little, knowing he couldn't appear too eager to get to Terry's house.

It was Angela West who had approached him on the way to school that morning. "Hey, Scott," she had called to him from the corner. "There's a party at Terry's today after school if you want to come."

That was all she'd said. She trotted off across the street to catch up with her friends. They looked back and giggled as they headed to the junior high school in the opposite direction of Johnson Elementary.

"Far out," Scott had said under his breath. He'd watched her walk away in her short skirt and tight sweater. *Maybe not the prettiest ninth grader at Las Palmas,* he thought, *but she is, let's say, the most mature.*

He smiled to himself as he watched her in the distance. Why she invited him to a junior high party was beyond his imagination, but he wasn't going to ask too many questions.

After parking his bike inconspicuously behind a tree, he ran his fingers through his hair and approached the house that looked like all the other houses in the neighborhood. Dandelions blowing in the breeze on the brown, weed-infested lawn gave away that Terry's parents were not into appearances.

Blond Angela answered the door with a beer in one hand and a cigarette in the other. At fourteen, she could have easily been mistaken for a high school sophomore. She motioned Scott to come in but said nothing. He walked down the narrow hall into the family room at the back of the house. There he found about ten kids sitting around on a green shag carpet next to an eye-popping orange floral couch.

"Hey," he heard Terry shout at some kids passing a joint. "My folks will smell that for days. Take it outside."

Scott casually merged into the group, moving out through the sliding glass doors on to the back lawn. He plopped down on the grass amid the group and took a hit as the joint passed to him. No one seemed to notice that he wasn't in their grade. His long blond hair was cool, and that was what mattered.

Someone in the group pulled out a bag of Doritos and passed it around. The chatter among the kids was silly and fun. Dumb jokes that were only funny after a few hits. Scott looked up to notice Angela motioning him to come in. He got up and moved toward her. He still didn't know what she was about, but he thought, *Better find out.*

She grabbed his hand and led him through the family room, then up the hall to a small living room opposite the front door.

They sat down on a formal, fancy-looking couch. Scott thought they were alone until he saw a couple making out in the corner.

With a pounding heart, Scott searched for something to say to Angela. Something, anything to seem not so nervous. Angela took a swig of beer and offered it to him.

"Thanks," he said as nonchalantly as possible. He took a drink and gave it back, trying not to react to the warm, sour beer.

She broke the silence for him. "I'm glad you came."

"Yeah, this is cool" was all he could think of to say.

Why did she ask me?

What difference does it make was the only answer he could come up with in the moment. He had met her the other night at the skating rink through another junior high school friend of his. They held hands for an exhilarating round or two around the rink, but he had assumed he'd never see her again.

She scooted in closer and turned to face him, inexplicably tilting her head, and kissed him on the lips. The weed from earlier had calmed his nerves and left him warm and relaxed. Why did it matter why she invited him? He kissed her back, swinging one arm around her and leaning them both against the couch.

She pulled away slightly, and Scott knew she was about to ruin the moment by speaking.

"You act older than you are, and you kiss better than any of the boys my age."

Her flattery was unfounded, but he didn't care. Thankfully, that was all she had to say.

The evening before the big game with Hagginwood, Marty sat at the kitchen table in his grandmother's house in Del Paso Heights over a plate of pork chops with bread stuffing. Ah, his favorite.

He suspected the pork chops were a ploy to loosen his tongue so she could give intel to his parents. They wanted to know what he was going to do with his life. He could hear the questions that probably came at her. "What's he going to do? Why is he killing himself with coaching and church groups? What's going on?"

She began the conversation casually. "How are you feeling about the game tomorrow?"

Marty shrugged. "Frankly, it could go either way. This has been a great season. I never expected to win so many games. Win or lose, it has given me a lot to think about."

"About what?" she asked.

"About my future. You know, what I want to do with my life. I'm thinking about the ministry, Grandma," he said.

"What?" she asked genuinely.

"You know," he said, "working with college kids, helping them through tough times in life."

She looked up from her plate and asked, "You mean being a coach?"

Marty swallowed a bite and tried to explain. "Well, life goes much deeper than sports. I want to help people with the spiritual dimension of their lives. Where there are real answers."

She shook her head slightly. "Hmm, your dad isn't going to like this."

The Jags sat motionless on the metal folding chairs in their own multipurpose room, watching the Hagginwood Hawks file in. They had been overwhelmed by Babcock, but this was a new level of anxiety. The all-Black team was decked out in new uniforms the colors of Grant High School—the school they would all one day attend.

The team watched solemnly as Hagginwood pulled balls out of black canvas bags and started their warm-up. Marty stood silently, searching the team for one particular player. Finally, he turned his attention to the Jags. He frowned when he saw Johnny chewing on his fingernails, Don tapping his foot erratically on the gym floor, and Bobby, ashen faced, looking like he was about to lose his lunch.

"All right, you guys," Marty began. "Heads up."

"Man," Bobby said out loud, "they are going to kill us."

His words said what each player was thinking.

Except for Penny, of course. "Oh, c'mon you guys. Just because they look big and really good doesn't mean we can't hold our own."

The rest of the team looked at her like they were trying to not roll their eyes at her delusional optimism.

"Penny," Johnny said, "you would say that if the Lakers walked in here today."

They all laughed, releasing a little of the tension.

"All right, listen." Marty got down on one knee in front of the team and lowered his voice. "Their best player isn't here tonight." He looked over at the team as they warmed up. "I heard he got suspended and sure enough, he isn't here, so that gives us a leg up, and we will take advantage of it."

He sent the team out to warm up and sat down to take another look at his clipboard. Johnson stood in a three-way tie with Hagginwood and McClellan. Hagginwood had lost to Noralto the week before, and because of that stunning loss to Johnson, Noralto got off their high horse and beefed up their defense, putting Hagginwood on their heels. As Marty predicted, Hagginwood beat McClellan, hence the three-way tie.

Marty had to remind himself, *this is sixth grade, not the NCAA*. But it still meant the world to all of them. He couldn't help but appreciate that after seven games, no one in the league would admit that Johnson was a team to reckon with, let alone that a girl dominated. That was okay. It would work to their advantage.

Seeing the Hagginwood team brought back some painful memories. He stared at the team, realizing this would have been his team if he had continued to coach at Hagginwood after the loss last year in the tournament. The injustice of the whole thing gnawed at him still. It had not occurred to him, until this moment, that he might find himself back in that tournament again.

As he watched, his attention focused on one player. When Marty coached the team, he had been a fifth-grade bench player. He was wild, elbows flying, even in the warm-up. This sparked a memory of the foul trouble that last year's team got in. Marty took mental note that getting this kid, number thirty, in foul trouble would be strategic.

Before the game began, Marty took Ramon aside and filled him in. "So here is the deal. You will guard number thirty. See him?"

Ramon watched the guy. "I'll bet he's their best player, Coach."

"Yeah, he is good, but he is out of control most of the time." Marty put his hand on Ramon's back.

"If you can draw fouls from him, you can make free throws, and maybe he will foul out early." Marty looked at Ramon, the one who always questioned his strategy. He looked for a flicker of understanding that he wasn't sure was there. "Be aggressive," he added. "Drive him to the hoop and draw the foul."

"Got it, Coach," he said. "You want me to harass him, make him mad, and then he will foul me a lot." Ramon grinned, his brown eyes widening in anticipation. "Yeah, sounds kind of fun."

Marty patted him on the shoulder. "Yeah, kind of fun."

The game started with both teams feeling each other out. Hagginwood felt the loss of their star player, and number thirty took it upon himself to make up the difference. His aggressive play and angry banter caught the attention of the ref.

Ramon played it cool at first, but scored off number thirty a few times, getting his dander up. After some choice words the refs didn't hear, and a few blocked shots, he had the guy flustered. Now it was personal. Normally, Ramon wouldn't intentionally tick someone off, especially a kid who was obviously a better ballplayer than himself, but he was learning all kinds of new things.

Marty watched as the team played with confidence against the presumably better team. All the skills he had drilled into them during practice were coming into play. They were good, they were having fun, and the score was even.

Scott dribbled the ball down the court, eyes darting back and forth at the defense. He watched the big guy whose body moved slowly and with hesitation. Scott darted around him and passed the ball to Ramon, who faked an overhead shot to the basket, pivoted left, and passed it back to Scott, who was now open. Scott caught the crisp pass, set his feet, and aimed for the basket. With the perfect amount of arc and spin, the ball hit the back of the rim and fell softly into the basket.

Hagginwood, astonished to see "surfer boy" do anything remotely athletic, finally realized they were up against it. Their in-bounder smirked as he passed the ball to his point guard, who carefully worked his way up the court to his own hoop. Eyeing the landscape for an open player, he failed to find anyone open because the Jags covered each of his teammates.

Seeing his only option, his left shoulder dropped, and he maneuvered the ball, dribbling toward the basket through the center of the key. Unaware of Scott's quick reach on the dribble, he batted the ball away in time for Johnny to snatch it up and prevent the drive. A clear bounce pass to Don on the outside of the key enabled Scott to break free and receive the ball to head for his own basket.

As the team came in for the half, Marty could barely contain his excitement. "You guys look great out there."

With the score very close, Marty turned to Ramon. "You've got him on the ropes, Ramon. Good job. He's got about ten points but three fouls. He won't last much longer."

Marty looked over at the Hagginwood bench and recognized the seething, sweaty face of number thirty. Marty commented to Ramon, "That was hard work out there, and it will pay off. Trust me."

Marty felt Mike tugging at his elbow.

"Coach, Coach," he made his best attempt at a whisper. "You should call the trick play. Call it, Coach."

"Not yet, Mike. Not yet," he said without taking his eyes off the game.

As the fourth quarter began, the whistle blew for the fifth time on number thirty. Their top scorer was out, and Penny came in with fresh legs to sub for Scott.

The embattled Hagginwood Hawks had learned nothing from earlier in the game and predictably underestimated Penny. She surprised them all by scoring ten points, leading her team to an impressive 30–25 victory.

The Jags went crazy. They leaped, hugged, and squealed with abandon. The small crowd that stood on the sidelines rushed the court and celebrated along with them.

The Hawks' coach, impressed by the win, understood—way too late—the Jaguars' secret weapon.

Later, at A&W, Marty felt the need to put things into perspective.

It was Mike who unknowingly set up the volley. "Coach, this is amazing! We could win the league! Can you believe it?"

Marty smiled. "Yeah, it is hard to believe. But I'm a little worried about McClellan. You remember what happened last time."

Mike looked up at Marty. "We should celebrate, and burn that bridge when we come to it. Right?"

Marty looked at his wise little friend and didn't have the heart to correct him. "Right, Mike. Today, let's celebrate."

Chapter 22

Sacramento, May 11, 1977
Four Days after the Murder

"**I didn't think much of** it at the time, detective." Sam, a local fisherman, took a seat next to Pete's desk. "I was on the river that morning, and I didn't want anyone to find my spot, so I walked down the road from my car to my favorite spot."

"When was this exactly?" Pete asked, admiring the elderly man who had the leisure time to fish in the early morning hours.

"Two days ago, detective. I think it was around six a.m."

Pete asked, "And what exactly did you see?"

"I saw these two guys get out of a car and head into the woods."

Pete nodded as Sam went on.

"Then this morning I read about them finding a body over that way, and I thought it was odd that those two guys were just walking around that deserted place. I never see anyone there that early in the morning."

"That is odd, Sam," Pete agreed. "Did they see you?"

"No, definitely not. They were headed up into the woods, and I was over by the river."

"What were they driving?"

Sam thought for a second. "It was green. A Toyota, I think. Kind of beat up."

"License plate?" Pete asked again, looking over the top of his glasses at Sam.

"Sorry." Sam looked down at his feet. "I didn't notice that."

"Did you get a good look at their faces?"

A sheepish look spread across Sam's face. "No, I didn't see their faces."

"What were they wearing, exactly?" Pete continued.

"The tall one wore a green coat. You know the kind you find at Army-Navy. I recognized it because I have one like that myself. The short guy had a sweatshirt with the hood pulled up. Dark blue, I think."

Pete scribbled down some notes and looked up again at the fisherman. "Did you hear anything? Were they talking?"

"Yeah, they were talking, but I couldn't hear much." Sam thought for a second. "Something about needing help and 'I'll owe you one.' Yeah, I remember hearing that. 'I'll owe you one.'"

"What is up that way—the way they were going?"

Sam answered, "Nothing much, just trees and scrub oak. Pretty desolate."

Pete asked a few more questions and thanked Sam for coming in. "This is helpful."

Sam stood and shook Pete's hand. "Glad to help, detective. Like I said, it just seemed a little odd."

After Sam left, Pete sat back down at his desk and rubbed his temples. He looked at his notes and compared Sam's story to the area where the body was found by the guy in the search party. If that was Jennings, down by the river, what was he doing there? Moving the body? Maybe he wanted to be the hero that day. It wouldn't be unusual for a killer to want to be the hero. "Maybe this was enough of a hunch to run a lie detector on Jennings, but that is about all," he said to himself while he reached for the phone and called DMV.

First, he checked title records for Dean Jennings. No car listed.

Next, he checked Jennings's cousin, who had been listed as a character witness in his previous criminal record. The guy owned a 1969 Toyota Corolla—green.

Chapter 23

Inconceivable

On the Saturday before the rematch with McClellan, Marty headed out the door with his golf clubs, hoping to calm his nerves. Hitting some balls at the driving range always seemed to help with stress. He walked down the sidewalk to find Johnny leaning against the Demon, staring at his feet.

"Hey, Johnny. What's up?" Marty asked as he approached the car.

Johnny shrugged. "Oh, nothing." The glum look on his face told a different story.

"Well, good timing." Marty opened the trunk, dropped the bag of clubs in, and slammed it shut. "Wanna go hit a few balls with me?"

Johnny, usually too cool, couldn't hide the pressure he was feeling. Marty was pretty sure it wasn't about the game coming up.

Johnny stood up straight. "Sure."

Still unwilling to fess up, Johnny jumped in the front seat and settled in for the trip to the driving range. The radio picked up in the middle of "Get Down Tonight" by KC and the Sunshine Band. It seemed a little too much for the moment, so Marty quickly switched the station. After a few more false starts, he settled on Elton John's "Fantastic."

Marty filled in the silence with chat about the upcoming big game. With little response, he simply said, "Swinging a club helps me with the stress."

Marty finally decided to shut up and let Johnny talk when he was ready. Johnny remained silent for the twenty-minute ride, looking like he was grappling with some deep unexpressed dilemma, and like he was annoyed with the music.

They drove down the familiar streets in silence. Many of the modest homes, built after World War II, had at the time been a sign of hope. The anticipation of fulfilling the elusive American dream had since disintegrated into run-down, overcrowded houses with iron bars on most of the windows.

There was a genuine feeling of community here, but most families struggled with low income, gang activities, and racism. It had been a few years, but the racial tension had reached its climax when Raymond Brewer was killed.

After they had hit a bucket of balls on the driving range, Marty said, "Hey, let's get a Coke."

They sat at a picnic table in the sun as they sipped from semi-cold cans of Coke from the vending machine. "Something eating at you, man?" Marty asked casually.

Johnny shrugged. "It's no big deal."

Marty chuckled to himself. *At twelve, everything is a big deal.* He remained quiet, hoping Johnny would open up.

Eventually, Johnny shrugged his shoulders. "The thing is, my cousins think basketball is stupid, except for Bobby of course."

Marty watched the boy's body language and knew instinctively the stress that opinions of the others could put on kids. "Do you think it's stupid?"

Johnny looked up and beamed for the first time that day. "No, Coach. I'm loving it!" He took a swig. "It's just that my cousin wants me to run with his guys. They drive around in souped-up cars and want me to run 'errands' for them. They're up to no good, but I could make some money, you know?"

Marty nodded. "Sure, I get it. It is a hard place to be at your age. Everyone wants to look cool and make some cash, too. The voices are loud out on the street." He paused for a minute then asked, "Did you ever hear the story of Raymond Brewer?"

Johnny frowned. "No, who is Raymond Brewer?"

Marty began the story about his friend from high school and the atmosphere that had pervaded the neighborhood a few years back. "I went to school with Raymond. He was an outstanding football player at Norte. He played varsity when he was a sophomore, and everyone knew he would play division one in college. He was that good." Marty stood and popped a few more quarters in the Coke machine.

"This is a two-can story," he said, smiling. "Do you have some time?"

Johnny sat upright. "Sure, Coach. Lay it on me."

"It was a typical Saturday night. Most of the high school kids went to Iceland on Saturday nights. You know, the rink over on Del Paso Boulevard."

Johnny nodded. "Yeah, I always wondered how such a weird place could be so popular."

Marty laughed. "When there is nothing else to do, that's how. Anyway, Raymond and two of his friends got a ride over there. They weren't going to go in and skate, just hang around outside with friends."

Opening the second can of cola, Marty went on with the story. "Raymond knew he would have to walk home, so he carried a broken-off broomstick with him."

Johnny looked at Marty. "Why?"

"Well, there were a lot of loose dogs wandering the streets. They were mean, and Raymond had gotten bit before, so he carried the stick around when he had to walk anywhere." Marty grinned at the memory. "And it looked cool, you know?"

"Yeah," Johnny said.

"So, Raymond and his friends get to the rink and hang around for a while with the rest of the kids. He was popular and everyone genuinely liked him. If he was on a football or basketball team, that team was a winner. If the team was a winner, then the school was a winner."

"I get the picture," Johnny said, relating to the story so far.

"When everyone went into the rink to skate, Ray and his two friends cut behind the rink into an alley and out into a dark intersection." Marty took a breath and seemed kind of solemn. "Just three blocks away, the boys heard shouting, 'Stop! Hey you, stop!'

"They couldn't see anything, but they heard voices yelling in the darkness. Their first instinct was to run. Assuming that they were not the ones being yelled at, they ran to avoid trouble. Right away they heard gunshots."

Eyes wide, Johnny gasped.

"The three of them, who had never been around guns before, kept running. Then Raymond collapsed. His friend Michael stopped and watched as the other kid, Adrian, ran back to where Raymond lay in the street. Adrian figured Raymond had tripped, so he ran back to help him. It didn't take long to realize he had been shot. Adrian bent over and picked him up. It had to be the adrenaline that enabled him to pick up Raymond and throw him over his shoulder and keep running." Marty gripped his Coke can but didn't take a drink.

"The boys were trying to get out of the line of fire. They didn't know what was going on in the street—no idea that they were the target."

Johnny sat mesmerized.

"You can imagine how scared they were. They heard, 'Stop!' again and then another gunshot. This time, Adrian fell to the ground with Raymond on top of him. Raymond had been shot again, this time in the back as he hung over Adrian's shoulder. The thud knocked the air out of Adrian, and he fell, scraping his face across the asphalt."

Marty stopped and took another drink while Johnny stared at him wide-eyed. "No way," he said in disbelief.

"Yeah, it's true." Marty shook his head. "Raymond Brewer, the nicest kid, the best running back Norte would ever see, lay dead in the street of a gunshot wound in the back."

All Johnny could say was "Who? Who shot him?"

"They were two plain-clothes cops. There had been a series of robberies in the area by three Black men with a sawed-off shotgun. The cops mistook the kids for the robbers, the broken broomstick for a shotgun, and running away for guilt. They never identified themselves as cops—just assumed the three Black kids were the suspects."

"That is so bad. Man, I can't believe it," Johnny said, shaking his head. "Did the cops go to jail?"

"No," Marty said. "In fact, they cuffed the two friends, and took Ray to the morgue in a body bag."

Johnny's mouth dropped open. "Man, that is the worst story I've ever heard."

"Yeah," Marty said. "So, the street fills with cop cars, sirens, an ambulance, and more cops than anyone thought Del Paso Heights had. And then," he added, "people started showing up, lining the street, wanting to know what happened. By the next day the community was really fired up."

"Heck, yeah," Johnny said. "They should have strung those cops up!"

"They gathered that night at the community center. There were hundreds that rushed out to be together and to decide what to do. They looked for someone to explain the meaning of this thing. Everyone wanted to know what they could do to get justice for Raymond's death."

"Were you there, Coach?" Johnny asked.

"The crowd gathered not far from my grandmother's place, so I saw it all unfold," Marty answered. "Everyone in Del Paso Heights knew about it."

After a pause, Marty said, "The crowd calmed down when they saw Raymond's dad move to the front of the crowd.

"It was nothing anyone had ever seen before," Marty said, shaking his head at the memory. "Raymond's dad stood staring out at the crowd with an intensity that lasted for what felt like forever. Everyone thought for sure he was going to rally that crowd to riot."

"Then what happened?"

"Here's the thing about the Brewers: they were a strong family. All the kids were star athletes and good students. Mr. Brewer was a commanding figure in the community."

"What did he say?" Johnny asked.

Marty remembered every detail. "He said, 'If you are going out tonight to do violence, do it in your own name. Do not use my son's name, Raymond's name, to justify your anger and hate. Do not do this thing in Raymond's name. It will not bring him back. It will not change this injustice. It will only make things worse.'"

"Geez," Johnny said, shaking his head.

"Yeah, the crowd went silent. This man they respected had not given them permission for violence.

"Their instinct for revenge unexpectedly softened. The crowd turned and went back to their homes. What had been a scary crowd had calmed down and slowly moved away.

"Raymond's dad said just the right thing to his neighbors," he said, working hard to hold back tears. "Raymond was my friend. I was devastated when he was killed. But it was his dad that had a huge impact on me. He spoke from his heart and averted a riot that night." Marty looked over at Johnny's brown eyes, wide in astonishment at the story.

"No moral to the story, Johnny," Marty said. "Just the reality of the world we live in. There is so much injustice and pain. There will always be pressure to conform to the passions of those around you. Living according to your own passions, like Mr. Brewer, is the tricky part. I would say, the better part."

Nearing the school for practice, Marty took a deep breath and tried to focus on the task at hand. *How do we prepare for this tough team?* Vengeance is a potent motivator after a humiliation like that first game with McClellan. The score of fifty-six to six rang in his ears like a fire alarm. Blood was running hot, but he knew it wasn't enough to beat the more advanced team.

He had drilled into these kids the basics of basketball the best he could. Having gone from hardly able to make a basket, they could now dribble with confidence, shoot with focus, and play as a team. Memories of their first practices brought a smile to his otherwise worried face.

On paper, McClellan was the better team, but he knew his kids played with heart. Did they just need dumb luck to win? A trick play or two? He could always pull out the clichés: "Just have fun out there," or "Play your very best, and you will do just fine."

A coach's patronizing pat on the head would not go over well with these kids. Marty felt sure they were sharp enough to see through the bunk. But he instinctively knew there was still good coaching to do.

He rounded the last corner to the school and noticed a few of the kids swing open the multipurpose room door. They appeared pumped-up and excited, but they had to be scared to death. Worst of all, he knew they looked to him for a win.

The practice started with the usual drills: layups, line drills, shooting, passing, and rebounds. He made them do the drills over and over.

"Come on, Coach," they protested as sweat soaked their T-shirts.

After an hour of drills, he called them in for a break. "Okay, guys, here is the thing." He looked at each player with more tenderness than he wanted to convey.

"McClellan on Friday for the championship. I want you to know how incredibly proud I am of you for coming this far, and I know you want to win." He paused again for effect and marveled at how much he loved these kids.

Starting again, he said, "These guys are going to be tough. It surprised them that we won so many games, but I'm pretty sure they will be ready for us."

"We will be ready for them too. Right, Coach?" Don said.

Marty looked at Don and the rest of the team. A memory from his own sports nightmare flashed before him as he remembered the dread he felt before the bout with Larry Jinks. Fear, sheer terror, was what he remembered. He didn't want these kids to feel that way about sports.

"I want you guys to give it all you have on Friday. All you have. Let's put into practice what we've learned, play as a team, and most of all, I want you to be proud of yourselves. I want you to look back on this season and feel good about what you have accomplished." He paused again, trying to not sound condescending or foreboding. "Winning or losing does not define you. But, if you don't do your best, it will haunt you."

He looked out at the earnest faces that stared back at him. "Does that make sense? Do you know what I'm trying to say?"

There was an uncomfortable minute or two, then a lone voice pierced the silence. "I think you like us, Coach. And I think you want us to like each other and ourselves, no matter how the game turns out? Is that right?" It was Penny who saved the moment.

They looked at her with admiration, then chuckled.

"Yep," Marty said with a grin. "Exactly right."

Game day blew in with a rainstorm that pelted sideways all day. Marty drove the team to McClellan in his Demon and did his best to calm the nerves of his players. They arrived, climbed out of the car, and entered the small gym, surprised that the bleachers were filling.

Jaws dropped when the team spotted students, a few teachers, and Principal Gould from Johnson. Marty watched as each player searched the stands for their families. Don spotted his mom, Bobby beamed when he saw his mom and her sister—Johnny's mom—and of course Coach Marty's grandma. Scott knew his sisters wouldn't be caught dead at an elementary school basketball game, but it was official, they had a fan base.

Although the crowd was gratifying, Marty prayed for the hundredth time that day. *Help!*

McClellan entered the gym to typical fanfare while Johnson sat on their bench and watched. Instantly, they remembered the uniforms, the coach, the players, their own humiliation.

"I can't believe we agreed to keep playing after that game," Scott moaned.

Marty was quick to get the team on their feet and out on the court. The typical warm-up brought familiarity and confidence as they moved the ball around the half-court.

"Eyes on the ball," Marty shouted when he noticed eyes wandering over to the opponents' warm-up.

Ignoring his own advice, Marty glanced over at McClellan's coach. His face clouted smugness that spread across the court like a dense Sacramento River fog.

It was clear from the beginning; this was all-out war. Game faces were stern and void of emotion. The usual smack talk had been replaced with determination. The tip-off went to McClellan, but the Jags started the game with energy that surprised the home team.

Both coaches paced the sidelines, locked in battle, voices hoarse before the second quarter started.

Mike stood next to Marty, elbowing him to get his attention. "Is it time yet, Coach?"

"Not yet, Mike, not yet."

Three seconds left in the first half saw Marty fight back tears. Tears of pride. He knew if the game was over now, it would be enough. As the halftime buzzer sounded, the team stumbled off the court to the sidelines. The sweat rained off foreheads, hair drenched, hearts pounding in their chests.

Having fought valiantly, the score was tied: 20–20. They had scored the most points they had ever scored in one half. They were fast, accurate, and relentless. How could they keep it up? Two more quarters was the question that rang through their heads. Two more quarters?

Taking a minute to compose himself, Marty spoke with a hushed tone. "You guys are playing with so much heart. I am so proud of you. I know you want this. I want it too. All I can say is keep doing what you are doing. You are putting into play everything we've learned together. Leave nothing on the court. It really is a thing of beauty. A real thing of beauty."

He paused and caught his breath. "My guess? They were not quite expecting you to be so much better than last time. But they do now, so it is only going to get harder."

Looking again over at the McClellan coach, Marty noticed that his confidence was now a sort of panicked "oh no" look.

"Oh, no" is right, Marty thought.

Focused back on the team, he said, "Okay, guys, here's the plan. Our best shot at winning is our defense. We have to stop them from scoring. Let's get scrappy out there. Scott, use your speed to keep up with the ball and put pressure on. Have that ball always in your sights. Don and Ramon, rebound, rebound, rebound. Get as close to the basket as you can and rebound everything. You guys could block some of those flat shots as well. Johnny, I'm depending on you to get your hands on the ball when they pass. Even if you don't steal it, you can tip it and mess with them, throw off their rhythm. That's what I mean by pressure. No matter who has it, pressure the ball."

Marty felt himself talking too fast as his adrenaline kicked into fight mode. He could taste this victory. They were so close. Taking a breath and slowing down, Marty smiled slightly. "Listen you guys, that ball in there, that is your ball. You own it. On offense, do your thing. Keep passing to open players. Penny is almost always open. On defense, all I can say is get scrappy!"

The players zeroed in on his instructions, watched with amazement as their coach's eyes glowed with intensity. They had come to a point where they actually "got it." They knew what he was saying and agreed with him.

"Second, we have to switch up our defense, catch them off guard. They are used to our man-to-man." He paused, eyes widening with urgency. "But at the right time I will call 'red' and I want you to switch to zone defense. Can you do that? We want to confuse them, but I don't want you to be confused. Can you switch like that, when I call it?" Marty looked around and watched their twelve-year-old brains connect to the concept. "Like switching gears on your bike, right?"

Don spoke up, "None of us have ten-speeds, Coach. But I think we know what you mean."

"Right, let's say like downshifting on a manual transmission. You know what that is like, right?"

Johnny laughed. "Yeah, Coach, we know what that is like."

"Now guys. This is risky, because if there is a hole in our defense, they win. But I think you can pull this off. I know you can. God knows you kids are smart," he said, practically under his breath.

Marty stood still for a minute and tried to see if the strategy was penetrating.

It was Ramon who spoke up. "Coach, that point guard is killing us. He passes to his wing, then the wing passes back to him, and he scores at will. I think we should let him make the first pass then pressure the ball and not let it get back to him." His eyes were wide and clear as he conveyed his idea. "Does that make sense?"

Marty could hardly believe his ears. "Heck, yes! It makes sense. Do it, for sure do it." He sent them back out on the court with a rush of emotion that took a minute to get under control.

As the third quarter got underway, Marty watched the pace of the game intensify. He was amazed to see his team of misfits play like pros. Well, maybe experienced seventh graders. They were focused, intense, and showing a level of skill that shocked everyone watching.

Then, halfway through the third quarter, Marty called the zone defense. It took only one trip up the court for the Jags to send the McClellan's offense into total confusion. The feeling of space to pass without the usual player in their face quickly deteriorated into wild passes and poor movement choices. The zone defense was quick to pick off the ball and, astonishingly enough, know how to work the ball back up the court to make a basket.

Parents and classmates, surprised to realize how good the Jags had gotten, were screaming their heads off. Scott was flying. Ramon was on fire. Don was a brick wall on defensive. Bobby was steady and focused, and Johnny was flawless. Penny was...well, she was Penny, who never missed a shot.

When the quarter ended, Marty blinked back tears as he looked at the scoreboard, thrilled with a two-point lead.

Mike tugged on Marty's sleeve. "Coach, is it time yet?"

Marty didn't look down at his manager but answered decisively. "Soon."

Late in the fourth quarter, Marty called a time-out during the Jags' own possession. Marty gathered the team at the sideline and spoke to Johnny. With a hand on his back, Marty gave him instructions. A minute later, he walked over to Bobby on the bench and spoke something nonchalantly that no one else heard. When the time-out was over, the ref gave Johnny the ball under the Jag basket for the inbound pass while Bobby set up near the free-throw line to receive it.

Then Johnny held the ball up and said, "Hey, Bobby, you take it out."

Bobby casually walked toward Johnny. "I got it," he said loud enough for the players on the court to hear.

The already flustered McClellan players let their guard down as they assumed he would trade spots with Johnny. As soon as Bobby got near the basket, Johnny passed him the ball, and he made a short bank shot into the unattended basket. The score recorded 32–28 Jags.

The McClellan players stood flat-footed and confused. "Wait, what just happened?" was written all over their faces.

The opposing coach hung his head briefly in frustration and disbelief, which instantly turned to anger as he shouted, "Come on!"

Marty watched the whole thing with satisfaction and a touch of retribution. He never would have used that inbound trick play except for the unconscionable run-up of the score by the McClellan team just two months before.

The Jags didn't skip a beat. They set up the press, got a steal, dribbled the length of the court, and made another quick two points, putting them up by six.

With fierce play for another few minutes, McClellan scored four points under the panic of the ticking clock and the din of screaming fans. Too little, too late. The buzzer sounded. Everyone in the room stopped cold and double-checked the scoreboard. The split second of silence exploded with cheers and screams of astonishment. The score, 34–32 lit up the scoreboard and the crowd went wild. The Johnson Jaguars had won the game.

The celebration escalated as the team jumped higher than they ever had playing basketball. They jumped, spun around, hugged each other, knocked each other over. What seemed inconceivable was a reality, and the joy coming from those kids was resounding. They had slain the giant. They had won the championship.

The McClellan fans sat stunned. Even though no one had thought it could happen, the Johnson Jaguars had earned the win.

Marty walked toward the McClellan coach with his hand extended. The coach took Marty's hand for the obligatory handshake with obvious reluctance and said, "You lucked out today, kid."

Marty, finding it difficult to speak, simply said, "Sure, Coach."

This time, the parents joined the celebration at A&W and Grandma footed the bill for root beer floats all around.

Chapter 24

May 9, 1977
Three Days after the Murder

A group of concerned neighbors drove to an isolated wooded area on the outskirts of Del Paso Heights and joined the local police in a search party. They stood tentatively at the edge of the designated area, waiting for direction from the police chief, who explained how they could help find a missing teenager from their neighborhood.

Their heads turned and considered the deserted woods only a few miles from their homes. Hoping they wouldn't find anything, hoping against hope that it was all a mistake.

After recording everyone's name and address, the police officers divided the crowd into small groups of eight people, sending away anyone under eighteen.

The chief cleared his throat with a little cough. "First thing to remember—touch nothing." He repeated the instruction. "Please do not touch anything you find. Use the camera we gave to each group leader. They will take a picture of anything that might be of help."

He walked to each group and handed the leader a grid map. "Stay in the grid of your map holder, take pictures, and mark them on the map if you see anything pertinent. Stay within your small group. Walk next to each other, arm's distance apart, walk slow but at the same pace."

The chief paused for emphasis, then spoke with authority. "Some of you have done this before—most of you have not. I must remind you to be vigilant, stay alert, stay in contact with your group leader. Each leader has a walkie-talkie. They can contact us anytime."

At last, he motioned to the officers to pass out brightly colored masking tape to each volunteer. "Mark stuff like broken branches, torn clothing, anything that looks out of place. Just put a piece of tape and keep moving."

The group had come to help but were terrified they might find something. The search party glanced sideways at each other, reluctant to get started. Eventually, they got organized and started to move with their grid leader and his map.

One man, tall and skinny, moved out ahead of the larger group. He muttered impatiently, "I don't have all day, let's just go." He didn't wait for the team leader, the map, the walkie-talkie, or the tape. Wearing a heavy green jacket, he headed right into the depth of the terrain, stepping over bushes, broken branches, and weeds. No more than twenty minutes passed when his voice rang out, bellowing through the woods. "Over here! Hey! Over here. I found something!"

As the sun went down and darkness closed in, the police car lights blazed and lit up the area around where the body lay. Stragglers from the search party couldn't tear themselves away, as if they were part of the case, characters in the drama.

"That guy that found the body?" one neighbor said to his friend. "That's Dean Jennings. I can't believe he even came out here. He's not your typical humanitarian type."

Police officers moved the crowd back as additional law enforcement, the coroner's van, news reporters, and more lights and cameras made their appearance. They should have gone home, but they stayed glued to the eerie, chaotic scene.

Chapter 25

Ankle Breaker

Marty threw open the front door, sprinted through the living room, bolted into the kitchen, and snatched the ringing phone off the wall mount without a second to spare.

"Hello," he said, trying to catch his breath.

"Yes, hello?" said an unfamiliar voice. "May I speak to Marty Brown, please?"

"Yeah, this is Marty." He looked around the floor for signs of Perky, afraid he had forgotten to put him out. *Hell to pay*, he thought.

"Uh, yes," came the reply. "I am the administrator for the Nor-Cal Champion's Tournament."

Marty's attention immediately returned to the call. *Now what*, he thought, but answered instead, "Yeah, how can I help you?"

"Congratulations on your team making it into the tournament. You pulled off quite a turnaround." He cleared his throat and continued before Marty could say thank you. "I'm calling to inform you of a few clarifications of the rules before the tournament."

Marty clenched the keys in his hand in response to the word "clarifications." This couldn't be good. "Thanks, uh . . . I'm sorry, I didn't get your name. What rules are we talking about?"

"Yes, I need to inform you that our rules clearly state that girls may not play in the tournament. I believe you have a girl on your team. Is that right?"

Marty didn't notice his keys digging into his palm until they'd reached an alarming depth. "What rule? What are you talking about?"

The voice on the other end of the line grew intense. "I'm sorry to inform you, Coach, but there will be no girls in this tournament." He didn't wait for an answer. "You are still welcome to participate, but we will not allow your girl to play."

Heat rose in his neck, and Marty yelled into the phone. "My girl? My girl has a name. Her name is Penny, and she has played all season. What do you mean she can't play!"

"No need to get belligerent, young man," he said with intensity. "It is the rule."

"I can't believe this!" Marty shouted. "There is no rule. If there is, it's like, what, ten minutes old?"

"It doesn't matter how old the rule is. She can't play," the administrator said flatly.

"Wait a minute." Marty's voice grew louder. He held the receiver away from his ear and shouted at it as if he was an inch away from the official's face. "So let me get this straight. Last year the refs stole the tournament from me, and now you won't let my best player play because she's a girl? You aren't going to let your refs have the pleasure of fouling her out in the first half?"

There was a momentary pause. "Well, I can see that you still have an anger issue, Coach. We could just as easily not let you in our tournament. Now, you go and have yourself a nice day."

The line went dead, and Marty listened in disbelief to the dial tone reverberating in his ear. The keys flew across the room, then slammed into the kitchen door, causing Perky to whimper against the wall.

Marty walked over to the school that day in grim agony. *How will I tell them?* He wondered out loud as he fought back his rage.

He wanted to kick something or hurt someone. *Those arrogant, self-important cowards. They are nothing but pompous, heartless cowards. That is all they are.*

"Hey, Coach!" He heard Penny's voice call out to him from behind. "Wait up."

Marty stopped and turned to see Penny running to catch up with him. He couldn't help but smile at her familiar freckled nose and wide grin under the too-big A's baseball cap. His stomach churned.

Their short walk to the school ended with Penny's tears spilling down her face. They would tell the team together.

Gradually, the team filed into the multipurpose room that had become a kind of sanctuary. They were excited. They teased each other, and laughed, with high fives in anticipation of another big win.

"Hey, Coach. We are going to win this tournament! Huh, Coach? We could win it!" they exclaimed as they made their way over to Marty, who sat with Penny on the multipurpose room floor.

Mike added to the excitement. "We should come up with another trick play, Coach."

"All right, everyone. Gather around." Marty motioned for them to come sit down with him and Penny. He waited for them to settle, took a deep breath, and started in. "I'm sorry, guys. I have some bad news. I hate to tell you this because it stinks, but here it is."

The team glanced over at Penny and noticed her head down and her cap pulled over her forehead.

Marty took a breath and watched as the expressions on their faces softened. "I got a call from some guy from the tournament. He says Penny can't play."

Audible gasps from the team hit hard like fists pounding against his chest.

"I am so sorry. There's some stupid rule, and they won't let girls play."

The disbelief hung thick in the air.

"Oh, no way!" It was Johnny who broke the uncomfortable silence. "If she ain't playing, I ain't playing."

The other players looked at him with caution and then eventual agreement.

"Yeah, Coach. She is part of our team. We wouldn't be here without her." Bobby declared.

They looked at their coach with a desperate desire for wisdom.

Marty cleared his throat, holding back emotion. "I thought you might feel that way, but I want you to sleep on it. Tomorrow, you can make your decision. Let's meet here after school, and you can let me know as a team if you want to play."

The group stayed on the floor, not knowing quite what to do. Slowly, they stood up, patted Penny on the back, walked out of the multipurpose room, and reluctantly went home.

That night, Marty tossed and turned as sleep was impossible. He stared at the ceiling. *What can I do?* He flipped around, buried his head in the pillow, and tried not to think about it at all. On one side, he stared out the window and struggled to lose himself in the night's blackness. On the other side, he finally fell asleep and dreamed.

The gym was completely full of screaming fans and parents. A band played "Louie, Louie." Cheerleaders in short skirts waved pompoms, shouting encouragement to the crowd. A TV camera moved in close to catch the pithy commentary of Marv Albert, clad in a plaid jacket, clenching a microphone. Marty was on the sidelines, in a suit and tie, pacing back and forth, hollering at blind refs and patting players on the back.

The team was older, in high school or college. He felt the familiar racing heart and made the quick scoreboard checks. Down by one, up by one, up by three, up by one, down by one, then up by one. The buzzer blasted, signaling the end of the game. The team jumped wildly, knocking each other over, screaming, smiling, sweating, laughing.

There was joy and fullness in his heart that was overwhelming. He was full, or almost full. Something was missing, and he was searching. His eyes scanned the crowd. He checked the bench. He looked around again with a sinking feeling. Where was she? Penny, where was she? He felt the victory, the joy of winning it all, seep out of his soul. But where was she?

The next day, after a restless night, the team met after school. It was unanimous. No Penny, no tournament. Their miracle season was over.

Marty cleared his throat and spoke with a shaky voice. "I thought after the McClellan game that I couldn't be prouder of you guys." He calmed his emotion. "I was wrong. I am prouder of you for making this decision to stand by your teammate, your friend."

With a wave of his hand, Marty herded the dejected team into his car. They squeezed in tight and set off for one more celebration. It was A&W instead of the tournament gym on the other side of town. Marty splurged on burgers, fries, and a round of root beer floats. They sat silently, not sure what to say or do.

"I'm sorry, guys," Penny finally spoke up. "You should play anyway. You've come so far. I'm so sorry." Her head hung low as she sat, dejected.

Marty resisted the need to enter in. He instinctively knew the boys needed to express themselves somehow.

"I won't lie," Don started. "I wanted to win that tournament and show all those snobs how we play. But it just isn't worth it to me to only take part of our team."

"Yeah." This time it was Johnny. "I don't want to play in their stupid tournament. They are afraid of us. Can you beat that? They are afraid of us!"

They were all nodding now, and Ramon calmly added, "Some things are more important than winning. Some things are just more important."

Marty smiled, and his heart filled with pride at these kids who had, in one season, done some impressive growing up.

Chapter 26

Heart Breaker
Sacramento, May 1977

Two years after that amazing season with the Johnson Jaguars, Marty sat at the dinner table with his grandmother. He had been house-sitting across town, studying for finals, for the last week. It felt good to have a home-cooked meal despite the awkward conversations about whether he should move back home to finish his last year of college.

At that opportune moment, the doorbell rang. Marty and Grandma both turned their heads in the direction of the front door. "Who could that be at dinnertime?" Grandma said.

"I'll get it." Marty got up and prepared himself to chase off a salesman.

He opened the door to see a man standing there dressed in a suit and tie with a somber look on his face.

"Can I help you?"

"Yes, I'm Detective Pete Willover, Sacramento PD." He held out his credentials for Marty to see. "I'm looking for Marty Brown."

Marty felt a dread he couldn't explain. "Yes, I'm Marty. How can I help you?"

Detective Willover cleared his throat. "I'm afraid I have some bad news. Can I come in?"

Marty opened the door all the way and let Detective Willover into the living room.

"Grandma," he called. "There is a policeman here." By now his imagination had assumed something had happened to his dad. *This is going to be bad* he thought as he invited the detective to sit down.

Grandma joined them, sitting next to Marty on the couch across from the detective.

Marty asked anxiously, "What is it? What has happened?"

"I was told that you coached a basketball team a few years ago. The Johnson Jaguars? Is that right?"

Marty's brow tensed with concern. "Yeah, that's right."

Detective Willover leaned in and spoke with care. "I'm sorry to tell you this news but Penny Parker went missing a few days ago and has been found murdered."

Marty and Grandma gasped at the same time.

Grandma said excitedly, "What? Murdered? Who would murder Penny?"

"I know this is shocking. It is so hard to believe, but we wanted to let you know and ask a few questions that might help our investigation."

Marty sat dazed and unable to speak. He buried his head in his hands and tried to process the information. Grandma looked at him with anguish. "Are you all right, son?"

"Yeah, I guess so. I just can't believe this."

"I wanted to ask if either of you had seen her recently. Anything unusual, strangers around, anything that might help us find who did this."

Marty lifted his head and blinked back tears. "I've been gone for the last week, house-sitting for some friends. I didn't even know she was missing."

Grandma spoke up. "She comes around on her bike once a month to collect for the *Bee*. But I haven't seen her lately."

Willover nodded. "We believe that she went missing on her

route a few days ago. We had a search party out looking, and that is when they found her. I'm so sorry to have to deliver this news. If you think of anything that might help, please call me."

He handed them his card and stood to leave. Both Marty and Grandma sat motionless and watched the detective walk out the front door.

Marty looked over at the little table against the wall and saw the newspaper wrapped in its rubber band. He stood and reached for it, unfolded it, and saw the story glaring up off the front page in bold black letters.

Girl, 15, Found Slain in Gully at Park Site

Above the headline, an eerie photograph showed several officers silhouetted against a flood of lights in a wooded area. Included in the headline, a detailed map of the neighborhood with an ominous X marking the spot where her body had been found.

He stared at the headline and the ghostly picture, hoping it was some kind of mistake.

A week later, on a Tuesday afternoon, four hundred and fifty kids solemnly walked into the gym at Las Palmas Junior High School. Marty watched as they filed in, assuming they didn't know what to expect from this assembly called after the inexplicable death of their classmate and friend.

They climbed the well-known bleachers and sat down heavily on the wooden planks they had sat on countless times before. *Even in the familiarity, they have to feel like aliens on foreign soil,* Marty thought. He knew he did. He also knew they were looking to the adults to make sense of the inconceivable.

She had been one of them. One of them had died. Could Marty help them understand?

His own broken heart beat wildly. He didn't know what to say. The emotion was overwhelming. The tears hadn't stopped flowing since he had heard the news. Death of a child? How do you explain that? Where was a loving God in this? How did he convey the love and goodness of God to children, let alone to himself?

He prayed silently, sitting in the folding metal chair, waiting for his turn to speak. More like a cry for help—a plea for words to come from outside of himself. The gym, a place that had already shaped him, would today be a place that would define him.

When the sounds of shuffling feet and creaking bleachers quieted, the assembly started with thoughts from a few of Penny's teachers, Principal Gould from Johnson, and Penny's youth pastor. Finally, it was Marty's turn, and he rose and stepped up to the mike. They stared at him, ready to receive something that would make sense of the death of their friend.

"Thank you for coming," he said. His first words revealed his weak and heavy voice. He cleared his throat and started again.

"I'm not sure what to say today other than to share my thoughts and feelings as we all go through this together."

Pausing, he looked over the crowd and recognized a few faces, students he had coached, the old Johnson team, teachers, and friends.

"I first met Penny a few years ago. She came into the gym with her ever-present A's hat on and asked if she could be on the Johnson basketball team." Marty laughed at the memory. "She turned out to be our ringer, our best player. If she took a shot, she never missed." He paused again and forced back the emotion.

"Penny lived down the street from me, and we often had good conversations. She was a deep thinker, beyond her years. Her losses and pain caused questions about life and death and what happens next. She was never shy or awkward about those things. She genuinely wanted to know."

The students sat still, not taking their eyes off Marty.

"I answered her the only way I knew. I believe only God knows the answer to those questions, but He is more concerned with us knowing Him than having all the answers. I believe, as did Penny, that He has made Himself known to us through Jesus."

The students remained silent. "Penny spent the last few years of her young life getting to know God, enjoying Him and serving Him, and now she is safe with Him.

"None of us know when our time will end. Penny certainly didn't. But she spent what time she had enjoying her family, her friends, sports, choir, and church. She enriched the lives of all who knew her."

After another pause, Marty looked down to gather his thoughts and wipe the tears that made it difficult to speak.

"I guess I would encourage all of us to live like Penny did. She had a lot of sadness, but it was her faith that gave her life meaning and purpose. I'm guessing she had a few questions for God, and I am sure He is answering them all."

Chapter 27

Overtime
Sacramento, 1980

The hot summer Sacramento sun beat down on Marty with ferocity. In late August, the sun had done its worst, and the usually lush green fairway was patchy brown and bone dry.

He set up his tee, positioned the ball, and swung the last drive of the day. After eighteen holes in the relentless heat, most would have quit a long time ago, but not Marty. He enjoyed the heat, and golf in the heat was even better. It was life-giving and energizing.

Maybe it was the precision of golf. Maybe the satisfaction of massacring that little ball that seemed to go further in the still, hot air. More likely it was the solitude that calmed his soul. At the least, it was the one area in his life where he felt successfully patient.

After the solitary round, he threw his clubs in the trunk of his post-graduation Plymouth Duster, slammed it shut, and set out across the road to a 7-Eleven for a cold Coke.

The arctic blast of conditioned air cooled him as he walked over to the fountain drinks. He grabbed a twenty-ounce Big Gulp cup, filled the bottom with Coke-flavored Slurpee, then finished it off with regular Coke. A traditional concoction for the drive home in the stuffy, torrid heat.

Marty approached the counter as the front door swung open, ringing the little bell, alerting the clerk that someone had entered. Marty recognized, out of the haze of five years, David Ramon.

"Coach!" Ramon cried. "Hey, man. How are you?"

Marty smiled and approached his old friend from the Johnson team, now almost as tall as himself. "Hey, Ramon. Good to see you."

They embraced, patting each other's backs with vigor.

"Look at you, man!" Marty said. "Geez. Are you, like . . . eleventh grade now?"

David grinned, his deep brown eyes sparkling. "Yeah, a junior this year. No one has threatened to kick me out since . . . well . . . sixth grade, man."

They both laughed knowingly.

Ramon glanced at the woman behind the counter. "This guy, man, this guy saved me," he said as tears brimmed. "If it wasn't for him, I'd be in jail. Heck, I'd be the guy coming in here to rob you instead of buying toilet paper to teepee my girlfriend's house."

Marty laughed. "Still the delinquent, huh?"

Ramon, filled with unexpected emotion, said, "Thank you, Coach. That season changed my life. In so many ways, thank you. What about you, Coach? Did you ever graduate? Any NBA prospects? Still driving that Demon?"

This time, it was Marty who grinned. "I did. Graduate, I mean. I even got married. And I got a new car. Not new really, but newer."

"No kidding? You found someone willing to marry you? It must have been the car."

"Definitely the car. We are here visiting Grandma. We moved to Montana of all places."

Marty asked, "Do you ever see anyone from the team?"

"Here and there. Johnny and Bobby are still in the neighborhood and doing okay. I still think about Penny a lot," Ramon said, choking up for the second time. "Penny. Our sweet Penny."

A surge of emotion made it hard to speak. Marty took a minute then said, "You are a good man, Ramon. It was my privilege to be a part of that amazing team."

After a few more minutes of reminiscing, Marty put some change on the counter, gave Ramon another hug, and said, "Good to see you, David. Keep up the good work."

Author's Note

On a smoldering Sacramento summer day in 2010, Marty and I were driving around in a borrowed car with no air conditioning, checking out his old neighborhood in Del Paso Heights. He showed me his grandmother's house on Santiago Street, Penny Parker's house, and other spots that prompted memories, sad and happy, of that spring in 1975.

"Show me the school," I asked, knowing it was close by somewhere.

We turned off Santiago Street and rounded a corner, then Marty slammed on the brakes.

"Wow," he said in astonishment.

We were staring at an overgrown field of weeds, edged by a cracked and warped strip of asphalt. We sat in the car, dumbfounded by the sight. The school had completely disappeared, leaving only weeds and a lone metal pole that once held a basketball hoop. The school, the multipurpose room, the sports fields, all gone. Dead grass, matted weeds, and painful memories made the place feel like a graveyard.

That summer day, we could only guess at what had happened. How does an entire school just disappear without a trace? I started digging to find out.

Thirty years after Marty coached the Johnson Jaguars, another great comeback story took place. The school, slated to be torn down and the population of students distributed across the district, unearthed a solution.

Enter a group of parents who would not have it. For a school struggling with underachievement, poverty, gangs, and racial tensions, they were seeing some improvements since the hiring of a new principal. They had even received grants from the Healthy Start program. The parents did not want those advances to be minimized or interrupted, and they certainly did not want to send their children to different elementary schools.

The fact that Johnson Elementary was built next to a natural gas storage facility gave the parents some leverage with the school district to relocate.

So, the fight began. With the energy of concerned parents, dedicated administration, and a history of spirit and pluck, the community saved their school.

Twin Rivers Unified School District spent $1.4 million to renovate an unused former junior high school nearby. The students of Harmon Johnson were, together, moved to their new home. The new school was in a safer location and provided the space needed to continue the innovative initiatives that were proving effective.

A few years later, the school won a prize that named them one of the three most improved schools in the nation. A trip to Washington, DC, to meet President Obama proved the value of a caring community and the advantage children have when they are the priority.

This story is a mixture of fact and fiction. The coach and most of the players are real. Some of the story has been changed and details filled in. Forty years after the fact, many names and particulars are remembered in hazy black and white, but much of what happened is still in brilliant color and has never been forgotten.

The story of Raymond Brewer is true. The racial tensions in the cities of America haven't changed enough for us to not still hear the gunshots.

As for women's issues, strides have been made, but it is still very dangerous to be a girl in the world today.

The details of the season are real. Athletics are as formational for young people today as they were in 1975.

The murder of a teenager committed in Del Paso Heights in 1977 is as true as it is tragic. This book tells one story of how DNA analysis became a game changer in investigating cold cases.

Detective Pete Willover is a real-life hero, and as of this writing, lives in the Sacramento area in retirement. Many of the details of the investigation are fictionalized but the results are actual.

The history of Johnson Elementary School is inconceivably and beautifully true.

ORDER INFORMATION

To order additional copies of this book, please visit
www.redemption-press.com.
Also available at Christian bookstores,
Barnes & Noble and Amazon

Printed in Great Britain
by Amazon